A CANDLELIGHT ROMANCE

CANDLELIGHT ROMANCES

DAZZLED
BY DIAMONDS

Phyllis Kuhn

A Candlelight Romance

Published by
Dell Publishing Co., Inc.
1 Dag Hammarskjold Plaza
New York, New York 10017

Dell ® TM 681510, Dell Publishing Co., Inc.

ISBN: 0-440-11710-0

Printed in the United States of America

First printing—January 1981

For my sons,
Murphy and Mike

CHAPTER I

She had pale blond hair and a slim figure and she strode out of Schiphol Airport terminal building into the crisp, clear Amsterdam morning, trailing assurance like a red balloon. Around the taxis at the curb, the huddled few eyed her advance. The women straightened and the men pulled in their stomachs.

Ordinarily Samantha Malloy would have arched and preened, given the folks their money's worth (adulation being meat and drink to any red-blooded cover girl), but this morning her attention was fixed on the time. For the fifth time in as many minutes she checked her watch. Six thirty. Right on schedule. She adjusted her dark glasses and moved briskly after the porter, who led her to her taxi as though heading a royal procession.

She fished a slip of paper from her handbag and showed it to the elderly cabdriver. "You take me this address?" she said in that oversimplified way some people talk with foreigners.

The cabdriver nodded. "Ja, Juffrouw." His lively blue eyes didn't miss a thing. "Amerikaans?" he asked, settling her small overnight case at her feet while she dealt with the porter.

"Canadian," she said and flashed thirty-five hundred dollars worth of orthodonture that dismissed the porter and at the same time signaled that she was ready to go.

About half an hour later the driver slowed along the canal-lined, tree-bordered street they had been traveling on. He maneuvered around a taxi pulling away from a trim little hotel with a Victorian facade. A short distance beyond he turned the corner.

He drove slowly, looking up the quiet street, past narrow, sleep-bound houses with pitched step-gabled roofs and scattered chimneys. Then, with an "Ah! Hier is het adres," he pulled up behind a battered blue truck, startling the two men huddled in conversation amid a tangle of mops and brooms at the rear of the truck. They were the only signs of life on the otherwise deserted street. Muffled in scarves and wool caps, they began coiling hoses busily.

Samantha paid the driver, ran up the short flight of stone steps, and tapped a gleaming brass knocker. She stood switching her overnight case and handbag from one hand to the other until the door finally opened. "Mijnheer VanDam?" she asked, stepping inside.

When she emerged thirty minutes later, carrying a handful of stamped envelopes as well as her handbag and case, the two wool-muffled men were still coiling hoses. She awkwardly closed the door and in the process dropped the envelopes. She quickly retrieved them and checked for damage. There seemed to be none. She hurried down the steps and headed for the corner, her footsteps echoing along the pavement. Pausing to deposit the letters in the bright blue letterbox, she then swung onto the boulevard and headed for the taxi queue at the little Victorian hotel.

Within an hour a departures clerk at Schiphol was returning her stamped passport. "Stay a little longer next time, Miss Malooly," he urged in a rich accent and with a big smile.

Miss Malooly. Mary Samantha Malooly. It sounded strange to her ears, though it was her real name and thus appeared on her passport. No one called her by it anymore though. Not since Grandmother Malooly died, the last link with her past.

"Mary Samantha Malooly?" the modeling agency

had said some years ago. "Much too country-kitchen, my dear. Perhaps a bit more *les salons*?"

A nip here and a tuck there and she had come up with Samantha Malloy, and everyone agreed it rolled off the tongue nicely. She seldom remembered it was not her real name. More than that, she lived up to its sleekness so successfully that nobody dreamed that within the elegant sophisticate there lurked a hobble-dehoy of a girl—Mary Samantha Malooly.

She gave the departures clerk a smile that had him sagging against the counter and headed for the departures lounge and the plane that would take her to the southwest of Ireland.

Right on schedule the jet climbed away from Schiphol Airport, made a slow, wide circle over flat, green fields, which were laced with canals and dotted with glass houses that glinted in the early sunlight; then leveling out, the plane headed for the North Sea.

In her window seat Samantha adjusted her dark glasses and watched the Netherlands slip away. She wore a pleased expression and a bra stuffed with fifty thousand dollars worth of diamonds.

She glanced down at the firm bulge across her front and congratulated herself. Everything had gone exactly on schedule. Just like clockwork. She settled back and relaxed, satisfied that she had performed her part well. It would be smooth sailing from now on.

Some hours later she would think back to that moment and laugh bitterly.

Circumstances had started to turn against her before she'd left Cork. The sky had clouded over and a fine gentle rain had begun to fall. Now, a half hour later, it was no longer gentle but hard and penetrating.

She gripped the steering wheel of the little hired car and wondered how much longer she was going to wander the narrow winding roads of Ireland before she found Parknasilla. Straining to see through the rain-smeared windshield, she cursed the hire-car fellow at Cork's airport. " 'Tis but an afternoon's drive to Parknasilla, and it's my very best car you'll be having for it," he had said, looking her straight in the eye and never saying a word about all the side roads a stranger could get lost on. And Samantha certainly had been doing a lot of that. The afternoon was long gone and still no sign of Parknasilla.

And if this was the best car, she pitied whoever had second best. It had balky windshield wipers, no heater, no radio, and dim headlights, and for the past hour the engine had taken to sputtering, coughing, and giving every indication that greater problems were on the wing.

She stirred uneasily. Being stranded on a dark and stormy night was something she didn't like to think about. Not with fifty thousand dollars worth of diamonds on her person.

She checked the firm bulge rounding out her coat front but with none of the joy she'd felt while tucking the cotton-wrapped stones into their silk pouches that morning. That feeling had begun to fade shortly after she'd turned away from the jet's window to relax and the woman in the next seat had zeroed in on her.

"Beautiful morning," the woman had boomed in a voice that could be heard across two fields and a water hole. Samantha had agreed that it was a beautiful morning, whereupon the woman pounced, "Ah ha! American!"

"Canadian," Samantha said without thinking.

"Ah, yes," the woman said, as though it made a difference. "Been in Amsterdam, have you?"

That was when Samantha had felt the first stirrings of suspicion born of sudden wealth. She gave the woman a wary look, her mind leaping to tip-offs and stick-'em-ups, and half expected to feel a gun poked into her ribs. People got riddled full of holes for a lot less than she had stuffed inside her bra.

But all the woman wanted was Samantha's ear, and this she filled with adventures of bird-watching around the world, until the plane touched down at Manchester, where she got off with a clanking of cameras and binoculars.

Samantha had then nervously eyed the boarding passengers, trying to look as though she had never heard of fifty thousand dollars worth of diamonds, and thanked God when two smiling-faced priests sat next to her. She had agreed it was a lovely day to be sure, said she was Canadian not American (bit her tongue over that), and when the priests disappeared behind their newspapers and books, she fell to brooding over how blithely she had promised to keep the stones on her person. Now they seemed imminently handy for greedy fingers. She told herself they'd go right into the hotel safe the minute she reached Parknasilla.

Now she sighed and peered through the windshield at the storm-ridden night. She caught herself squinting and stopped. Squinting made wrinkles. And wrinkles turned fashion models into ex-fashion models. She sighed again. Where was Parknasilla anyway? By now the other models, the photographer, and the crew would have arrived from New York.

"Three days of haute couture with an Irish background," the modeling agency had said, without knowing what a boost the assignment gave to removing the obstacle in the path of her becoming Mrs. Warren Beck. The obstacle was lack of money.

To be sure, Warren made plenty of the stuff as the fastest rising attorney to hit today's legal circles. But he had his eye on bigger things—a small political office for openers, and then something more important than that, and then something bigger, and then—well, why not on to the Governor's Mansion? And that was just a step away from Samantha Beck, First Lady, wasn't it?

But it would all cost lots of money, Warren had said. It was possible she had only imagined that Warren did not smile quite so brightly when anyone remarked what a beautiful couple they made—he, tall, dark, and smooth; she, tall, blond, and smooth. And there probably had been no basis at all for her thinking his eyes lingered long on heiresses despite their warts. Just the same he was back to arriving at her apartment early and leaving late since he'd turned her assignment into a stepping-stone toward his goal. Fourteen stepping-stones, as a matter of fact. Fourteen diamonds. Fifty thousand dollars worth.

"Fifty thousand dollars worth of diamonds on today's Amsterdam market, Samantha, will have a far greater resale value in Canada a year from now," Warren had said. Though why Canada and why a year from now Samantha had never got straight any more than she'd understood why she had had to take off from Canada instead of from New York. All that mumbo jumbo about being a Canadian citizen and Canadian customs laws and tax breaks. All she knew was that it meant a brimming cup for the future Warren Becks. At this time and distance, however, the thought didn't bring the warm feeling it usually did.

She was getting colder and more tired by the minute. If she didn't reach Parknasilla soon, she'd be in poor shape to face the cameras in the morning.

She cautiously applied some pressure to the gas pedal. Immediately the engine sputtered. She eased up and for a heart-stopping second the car stalled, then lurched and staggered on. She gave her full attention to the business of urging it down the narrow rutted road

12

and around the tricky bends and rocky promontories that jutted suddenly out of the darkness. In some places on the near side the land dropped straight down to where the sea crashed and foamed far below; in other places it was flat, and huddles of cattle and black-faced sheep drifted wraithlike out of unfenced fields, stopping in the middle of the road and blinking into her dim headlights. Always the rain beat steadily down.

So far Ireland was a big disappointment, not a bit like the stories Grandmother Malooly used to tell her. "A lovely place it is, Mary Samantha. The soft moist air and the mist-veiled mountains. And, oh, the green of it!"

Moist air is right, Samantha reflected gloomily. *Gallons of it.* On and on she drove as squally blasts buffeted the car and rain bucketed down. The car's ominous noises became more ominous. The dark lonely road took more of the bloom off wearing a fortune in diamonds. Warren had said she'd have nothing to worry about. "You'll find the people are simple, hardworking country people. God-fearing and friendly. There is practically no crime rate where you're going. Of course"—he had gone on to spoil it all—"there are the tinkers. . . ."

"Tinkers?"

"They're nomads who go about in rag-tag horse-drawn wagons, roaming Ireland, living by their wits. Begging and petty thievery. For the most part though they never give any serious trouble."

It was that "for the most part" that stuck in her mind as she coaxed the wheezing little car on, hoping Parknasilla was around the next bend. It wasn't. She tried to remember when she had last seen it mentioned on a road sign. A long time ago. It had been a long time ago, come to think of it, that she'd seen any road sign.

13

Or a village. Or even passed a car. She began to look forward to the next huddle of livestock.

And then, maneuvering around a turn, she saw the first sign of her fellow man in hours, but it did nothing to raise her spirits. As soon as her meager headlights picked out the barrellike wagon pulled off on a clearing, memory stirred. Tinkers? She fearfully eyed the caravan as she drew closer. A stove pipe stuck out the top. Pots, pans, and bits of iron were tied to the dilapidated sides. Tinkers, all right. Three or four swaybacked horses staked out to one side looked up, staring dumbly as she passed.

Holding her breath, her eyes alert for the first sign of attack, she prayed the little car on and gave shaky thanks when she slipped past without a knife-wielding brute-faced swarm of rascals rushing out of the night after her. Nonetheless she went a full mile farther before she breathed normally again, and she was still driving with one eye on the rearview mirror when she caught the flash of powerful headlights coming up behind. Coming up fast. One moment the little car was flooded with light and in the next, a sleek white Jaguar overtook her, spraying the windshield with mud. She glared after the disappearing blur of taillights. "Damn you!" she said in the voice of Mary Samantha Malooly, though more in envy than outrage.

She stopped the car and watched the now-and-again wipers shove the mud around. Finally she set the brake, prayed the engine would not die, and ducked out into the storm, trailing a stream of invective that would have made Warren's eyes bubble.

The wind whipped her clothes, tore at her scarf, and fought for the contents of her handbag as she groped for tissues. Then suddenly a fresh gust swooped down and the next instant a flurry of white went sailing off into the inky night. For a startled second she watched

14

the wildly scattering specks. Then, setting her jaw, she gave the muddy windshield a swipe or two and dashed back into the car just as it was gasping its last gasps.

She was wet, cold, very tired, and up to her thirty-five-dollar eyelashes with Irish weather, Irish countryside, and most of all Irish cars. Malooly shoved an elbow and a shoulder through the Malloy gloss and glitter. "You damned miserable piece of junk, don't you dare conk out on me." She banged the dashboard.

The lights flared bright, the wipers started a brisk *swick-swuck,* and the radio burst forth with a lively skirling of bagpipes. After an astonished moment she nudged the gas pedal. The motor sprang to life, and the little car took off like a Grand Prix winner.

Her spirits lifted, Samantha took a fresh hold on life. She twisted the dial for something other than bagpipes. "Now," said a bright chirpy voice, "in order to have a really good compost heap—" She turned out the bright, chirpy voice and tuned onto a grave British one. " . . . in Amsterdam, was discovered by his housekeeper—" The grave British voice joined the compost heap; so did a fiery Gaelic speech and a lively rundown of soccer results. She flipped back past the sports and the political harangue and stopped at the newscaster. ". . . and authorities are searching for the young woman," the elegant voice reported, then shifted gears. "And now for traffic conditions: There is a lorry down at the roundabout and a buildup is—" She twisted the dial back to the pipers and made herself comfortable.

The car purred along as though it had never had a problem in its life, and a mile or two farther on its bright headlights trapped a road sign. Samantha pulled up and peered out through the rain to learn that Riverford lay just ahead. Riverford? She got out her small flashlight and examined the map. There was no Riverford between Cork and Parknasilla. There was no Riverford anywhere around Parknasilla. She sat back and thought. But not for long. The weather being what it was, the hour being what it was, and most of all her energy level being what it was, Riverford became the bird in the hand. Parknasilla would have to wait in the bush.

She got underway again and presently came to a rickety old bridge stretching across a wide expanse of black rushing water. A weather-beaten sign announced that this was High River Bridge.

She took a long look at the bridge before putting the car in gear and moving onto it. Before she had gone a car's length, she realized she had made a mistake. But to back off in that soggy darkness, with the puny side rails giving no protection against winding up in the deep, seemed like choosing Scylla over Charybdis. She inched the car across the wobbling old planks, feeling them sag under the weight of the car and sensing the water lapping around the wheels. When she finally reached the opposite side, she was trembling and her hair was plastered to her brow. But she simply drew a tremulous breath and got underway again, driving slowly and looking for the lights of Riverford.

Breasting a rise, she was startled to find a tree growing directly in her path in the middle of the road. At her searching snail's pace it had presented no problem, but it did seem a peculiar place to have a tree. She pulled around it and there was Riverford, such as it was.

A handful of small shops loomed black and shapeless along the dark, rain-drenched road ahead. Closer at hand, a few feet off to her left, she saw in her headlights two low stone gateposts marking the entrance to a side road. One of the gateposts bore the shattered remains of a small sign that brought a cry of joy to her lips.

Tilted, splintered, and drunkenly swinging, it read, O'SULLIVAN HOUSE, REGISTERED AND FULLY LICENSED. And beneath it, lying in a ditch like a fallen giant, was a white Jaguar. Shattered bits of the sign were scattered on its hood, its right wheel and fender neatly crumpled into the rough stone and its left rear hanging in space.

Samantha swung onto the side road, checked for possible casualties, and pushed on to journey's end, gloating inwardly. Another blow struck for the tortoises.

CHAPTER II

About three quarters of a mile down the twisty, muddy lane, Samantha's headlights lit up the darkened front windows of a whitewashed stone cottage. Though it seemed small for an inn, what did she know about Irish inns? At least there was a glimmer of light at the rear of the cottage and none at all on the black rain-swept road beyond. If this was not O'Sullivan House, at least she could get directions to it.

She parked the car, ran through the driving rain up the cinder path to the door, and banged the knocker. The wind carried the salty tang of sea air. It mingled with the sounds of the storm and she could hear the faint boom of surf rising from somewhere behind the cottage.

In a moment a light wavered across the near window and the door opened. A figure loomed in the half shadow of a flickering oil lamp, his wiry black hair in wild disorder, his faded blue jeans and sweat shirt stained and rumpled.

She imagined her body lying in an Irish ditch and her diamonds scattered among the great unwashed. She took a step backward. "I—I'm looking for O'Sullivan's," she began.

"And you've found it," the fellow said, throwing the door open. "Come in, will you, come into the warm."

His smile was wide, his voice cheerful, and his manner as lively as a cricket's. Her fears eased. Peering beyond him, she glimpsed polished wood and soft green leather. From somewhere in the back she heard the opening strains of Mahler's Fourth Symphony. Completely reassured, she stepped inside. "I hope you have a vacant room," she said.

He hesitated for only a split second. "I have so," he declared and waved her on in. Setting the lamp down, he said, "I'll just be after getting your bags. You can be leaving your wet things by the fire, if you've a mind to." He motioned to a turf fire glowing in the grate and then sprinted out into the night.

A green leather sofa faced the fireplace. Flanking either side of it were two deep chairs. On one of the chairs was a man's wet muddy coat and an equally wet and muddy suitcase. An attaché case sat on the floor beside it. The driver of the Jaguar, she guessed. So much for the tortoises.

Half out of her own coat, she paused to take stock of the bulge straining the buttons of her suit jacket and gave a moment's thought to the stick-'em-up sort of thing. The fleeting thought fell apart on closer inspection however and she set her things to dry.

The door banged open, and the youth blew back in with the storm at his heels. " 'Tis a filthy night, for sure," he said, slamming the door and setting her bag down. He came over to the fire and handed her the car keys. "I've locked your car. 'Tis said there's tinkers gathering in the back hills."

"Anyone stealing that car might not get very far. It's a rental and not at all reliable. It gave me trouble most of today."

"Did it now? Would you know I've the very same model that's been giving me trouble too. It's in Killarney right now being checked over."

"Try banging the dashboard next time," she said, warming her hands at the fire and looking around the shadowy room. It looked more like someone's living room than an inn, she thought. There didn't even seem to be a registration desk, but perhaps the Irish did things differently. More importantly where did they keep the telephone? "If you'll show me where the telephone is, I'd like to make a local call—at least I hope it's a local call to Parknasilla. I'd hate to find I've lost my way too far off."

"Ah, yes, 'tis a local call but I'm that sorry—I've not got a telephone."

That certainly presented a problem. She could imagine the fur flying around Parknasilla when she didn't show up. Strange, though, an inn without a telephone. Or was it? In any case it meant she'd have to leave early enough in the morning to arrive before the photographer was up and started to yell about ruined shooting schedules. She certainly had no intention of trying to make Parknasilla anymore tonight just to keep tempers from flaring. She shivered at the thought of going into that weather again.

"Will you look at me standing here and you that cold! Would you be wanting a cup of tea to warm yourself? Or a drop of whiskey perhaps?"

A drop of whiskey would have hit the spot, but calories lurked therein, and Samantha had to battle to keep slim and leggy and ahead of the dewy-eyed youngsters making the agency files these days. "Tea will do nicely," she smiled.

"Come along, then, to the kitchen." The youth picked up the lamp. "The storm's knocked down the electric lines," he explained, leading the way toward the strains of Mahler.

The kitchen did not look like a commercial establishment either. Samantha noticed a cheerfully burning oil lamp, freshly painted white walls, and bold Matisse-like splashes of red, yellow, and blue in the curtains.

Another fireplace dominated the far wall, and in a bright red rocker to one side of it, half turned away, a man sat with his long legs and stockinged feet stretched to the glowing fire, his chin in one hand and a drink in the other.

He seemed to be brooding rather than absorbed in the music pouring from the transistor on the mantelpiece above him. At least so Samantha thought as she paused in the doorway. She had a habit of pausing in doorways to give people in the room time to recover from their first glance. At any rate the man didn't look around as the youth moved into the room.

" 'Tis another traveler that the storm's brought me," he said, setting the lamp down on a round wooden table.

The man half stirred.

"Another American like yourself, Mr. Carter," the youth continued. "Miss—" He turned and caught the full effect of Samantha posed on the threshold. His eyes bugged. "Wow," he said under his breath.

A glance brought Luke Carter to his feet and wiped away his brooding air. An expert eye took in the pale blond hair caught carelessly around the head. It assessed measurements and liked what it saw. "Well, well," he said in a pleased voice. His gaze settled on the well-stocked bosom. "Yes, indeed."

Samantha agreed with Schopenhauer that modesty was a lot of bunk promoted by those who had no reason to be otherwise. Then, increasing the wattage of her smile, she glided across the room with that boneless, gravity-defying glide of the model and held out her hand. "I'm Samantha Malloy," she said to Luke.

He took her hand in both of his. "Luke Carter," he said, the rustle of bed sheets in his voice.

He was somewhere in his middle thirties, Samantha guessed, tall and hard-muscled, with disheveled sun-bleached hair and a weather-beaten face. His nose looked as though it'd been broken at one time, and his jaw assured the other guy had fared worse. He had a wicked grin with strong white teeth and deep-set gray eyes that caressed her. For no reason the thought crossed Samantha's mind that a woman would have a hard time refusing him if he wanted her. Except for herself, of course. She had Warren. She tugged her hand free.

"And my name is Leibowitz," the youth said, stepping up. "Sol Leibowitz. Welcome to Riverford."

Luke pulled a chair closer to his. "Won't you?" he invited, and reached for a bottle of Scotch on the floor beside him. "We need a glass for Miss Malloy, Sol."

"I'm having tea, thank. . . ." Her voice trailed off and she frowned. "Leibowitz?" she said to Sol.

"That's right. Leibowitz. But will you be calling me Sol?"

She stared after him as he crossed the room to a small stove fed by some sort of bottled fuel. Then she turned back to Luke. "Leibowitz?"

He grinned and nodded. "Saint Patrick must be spinning."

Again she got that wary feeling that is so easily triggered when one is carrying the family bankroll. "Mr. Carter," she said in a low voice, "have you stayed here before?"

He tore his eyes from her bosom. "No, it's my first trip to Ireland."

She leaned closer. "This is sort of small for an inn, isn't it?"

He looked surprised. "This isn't an inn. It's Sol's house."

"Sol's house? But the sign . . . I asked . . . he said. . . ." She rose swiftly to her feet, drawing Sol's attention. "You said this was O'Sullivan House," she said accusingly.

He came back to the fireside. "O'Sullivan House? I thought you asked if this was O'Sullivan's—which it is. O'Sullivan's cottage. O'Sullivan House is up the road. Only it's been closed for a long time."

"But the sign said—"

"Ah, now, everyone knows O'Sullivan House is closed so no one's thought to take the sign down."

"Well, I certainly can't stay here." She gathered up her purse. "Where is the nearest hotel or inn?"

" 'Tis farther away than I'd want to travel on a night like this. What's wrong with staying here?" He looked to Luke for support.

"You wouldn't get me out again in this weather," Luke said. "Not if I had to cross that damned bridge the way it's storming now. Listen to it come down, will you." He settled himself more comfortably.

She considered the wind whistling around the corners of the house and the rain slashing at the windows, and her thoughts took a fresh turn. Did it make sense to wander around in all that weather, down lonely dark roads, looking for a place to stay? Particularly with tinkers in the area? She eyed the two men. It boiled down to a question of the devil you knew versus the devil you didn't. "Well . . ." she said.

"Good. That's settled," Sol said quickly. And when she reseated herself, perching indecisively on the edge of the chair, he pulled up a stool for himself. "Look, Miss Malloy, Michael O'Sullivan was my grandfather." He broke off to grin. "Maternal, that is. Anyway, grandfather was born in this cottage, and when he died a couple of years back, he left it to me. He left me O'Sullivan House too."

"Must've shocked the hell out of the natives," Luke said over the rim of his glass.

"They mutter darkly among themselves at the sight of me," Sol said cheerfully. "But my charm's getting to some of them."

Samantha looked around the cozy room. "You've moved here permanently?"

"I have that. Got me a girl here. She helped me fix

23

up this place and is helping me with my plans for O'Sullivan House." He leaned forward and stirred the fire. "O'Sullivan House was originally what the Irish call a Great House. Grandfather worked in its fields as a boy, and when he grew up, he went to America to make his fortune. When he'd done so, he came back to Riverford and bought the Great House, turned it into a hotel, and called it O'Sullivan House. It didn't make any money but he didn't care, it gave work to the villagers. I was in school when he died and pretty caught up in studying art. Riverford sort of got lost in the shuffle. When there was no one to take charge, the lawyers shut down O'Sullivan House. But now that I'm here, I'm going to make a sort of resort out of it."

"Need a tax write-off, do you?" Luke said.

"No, I'm thinking it'll go over now with all the activity on the coast. A lot of foreign industry is going in, as you know, being here to look the place over yourself. And Riverford's on a direct route—handy for a weekend's fishing and relaxation. I'm thinking foreigners will get a bang out of a real Irish manor house—complete with secret passages."

"Secret passages?" Samantha asked, taken with the idea.

"They say the gentry used them to duck rebels back in the Time of the Troubles." He got to his feet and smiled down at Samantha. "I'm glad you've decided to stay, Miss Malloy."

"So am I," Luke said, looking at her over the rim of his glass, his eyes making plans.

Samantha caught the ripple of muscles as he lowered the glass and, sensing the strength of his arms, found herself wondering what it would be like to go along with those plans, to feel the strength of those arms, the pressure of his firm mouth making demands against hers. Then, looking up, she found his openly amoral

24

stare still on her, and her heart began thudding in her ears. Quickly she looked away, dismayed at her reaction, feeling somehow she'd lost command of the situation. Striving to recover control, she flashed a professional smile at Sol. "You're a dear to take me in. My fiancé told me it was a friendly country," she said.

"Got one of those, have you?" Luke said, sighing a little. "Oh, well. . . ."

"Then it's daft the man must be, letting you go off alone, so far from his side. Do you not think so, Mr. Carter?" Sol asked, looking as though he'd not missed a thing.

"Daft," said Luke in a voice that unaccountably put Samantha back in the catbird seat.

"And now," Sol said, rubbing his hands, "the kettle will have gone cold. Can I fix you a sandwich while it gets to the boil again, Miss Malloy? Or would you like some cakes? Or biscuits?"

She would have liked a sandwich *and* cakes *and* biscuits. She was starving. She was always starving. It was no bed of roses being a model. "No, thank you. Just tea."

"Then would you be wanting a sandwich?" Sol asked Luke. "There's cheese and cold meat and I'm thinking I'll be fixing one for myself."

"Nothing, thanks. And by the way," he added dryly, "that's a hell of a thick Irish brogue for a Leibowitz of Beverly Hills. Don't the natives think you're putting them on?"

"Funny thing about that. It's this country. It takes over." He grew thoughtful. "Either that or Ireland claims its own. I don't know which. But if you stick around, you'll be doing it too, I'm thinking."

"I don't plan to stick around," Luke said, settling back to his drink as Sol returned to the sideboard. "No longer than it takes to get that car out of the ditch and my business over with," he told Samantha. "What a hell of a place for a tree. Right in the middle of the goddamned road. Riverford'll need a hospital more than a resort if they don't remove the thing once traffic starts coming through."

"I'm surprised you didn't wind up in a ditch long before Riverford, the way you were speeding when you passed me down the road."

"Did I pass you?"

"Just beyond that tinker's caravan. You splashed mud all over my windshield, and I had to get out in the storm and clean it off."

"The hell I did," he said with the right amount of contriteness.

"It's no matter now," she said good-naturedly. She sat back, relaxing. The rain beat down on the thatched roof and the fire hissed pleasantly. Mahler had long ended and Mozart now filled the room. Sol was humming while opening and closing cupboards and drawers. She gazed at the fire and let Luke drink his fill of her.

Eventually he stirred. "I'd say East Coast. New York"

She smiled. "By way of Canada." After all, where was the harm?

"Been in Ireland long?"

"No, I just flew in this afternoon from Amsterdam." She looked after the careless words. Now there, that was wrong. Warren wouldn't like that at all. He had said, "No one, but no one, is to know of your stopping over in Amsterdam, Samantha. Do you understand that?" And she had said, "Yes, Warren." She always said yes, Warren. But she hadn't understood. What did the diamonds have to do with his political future being ruined? Just the same she bit her lip.

"Nice place, Amsterdam," Luke said.

26

"I didn't see much of it," she said hastily. "I got in late last night and stayed right in the airport hotel. Actually, I was in the town itself for only a few minutes this morning on a bus—" She caught herself. Fortunately Sol came up with her tea. And not a moment too soon, she thought, seizing the cup.

"Watch it, it's hot," he warned, seating himself beside her and biting into his sandwich. He looked expectantly from one to the other, as though ready to join in their discussion.

Samantha grabbed the chance to change the subject. "And what sort of business are you here on, Mr. Carter?"

"Engineering contracting. I've sent a crew ahead, scouting those jobsites on the coast that Sol was talking about, and we're putting the bids together tomorrow. I hope you're headed in that direction. I may have to bum a ride."

"If it's on the way to Parknasilla, I am."

"It's in the opposite direction," Sol said.

"Would you consider taking a detour?" Luke asked Samantha.

She was tempted. She actually was. But common sense prevailed. "I'm sorry, but I have to be in Parknasilla first thing in the morning. Maybe Sol will drive you if you're stuck for transportation."

"Are you forgetting my car's in Killarney for repairs?" Sol said. "But don't worry, Mr. Carter. We'll just hitch up a horse or two to your car and it'll be out of the ditch and you on your way in no time."

"God, I hope so. The car belongs to a friend in London, and she needs it tomorrow night. And I've got to be on the job first thing too so I haven't any time to hang around waiting for some mechanic from Killarney to get here and fix it."

27

"We'd best be thinking positive, then," Sol said. "For I'm afraid it's unlikely there are even tires for a Jaguar in Killarney, let alone spare parts to repair it."

Luke frowned at that and sat pulling at his drink. Sol ate his sandwich. Samantha sipped hot tea and thought about the "she" as in "she needs it tomorrow night" until she became aware that a newscast had come on the transistor and the announcer was saying something about diamonds. This being a subject near to her heart, she listened more closely.

". . . the safe was open and the diamonds were gone and the room in complete disorder," the solemn voice reported. "The cabdriver told authorities he had driven the attractive blond to that address from Schiphol Airport about six thirty this morning. A search is now on for the young Canadian woman. . . ."

Samantha's teacup fell to the hearth, breaking into dozens of pieces.

CHAPTER III

Sol rescued her handbag from the spreading pool of tea, mopped up and gathered the broken bits of china while she made little noises of apology and moved her feet out of the way, carefully avoiding Luke's eyes. She was not at all happy with his look of sudden interest.

When Sol went for another cup of tea, Luke said softly, "Something in the newscast startle you, Miss Malloy?"

To admit he'd said a mouthful would lead to whys and wherefores she wasn't prepared to answer. "The—the newscast?"

"About that diamond broker. In Amsterdam."

"Why should that startle me?"

"Why, indeed?"

She could see at a glance that his manner had undergone a subtle transformation since the voice from Britain had drifted across the room. Though a trace of admiration still beamed in one eye, suspicion dawned in the other. Once more she welcomed Sol's arrival with tea.

He looked at her closely. "You okay, Miss Malloy? You look sort of pale."

She wasn't surprised. She felt pale. She mustered a smile. "It's been rather a long day. . . ."

"Would you be wanting to go to your room?"

Would she indeed! The past few minutes had provided a wide area for solitary speculation on what one does if one turns out to be the blonde the police were looking for. On the other hand she wasn't really sure she had heard what she thought she had heard, and the only way to find out was to stay put until the next

29

newscast threw more light on the subject. "I'll finish my tea and enjoy the fire a bit longer."

Sol nodded understandingly. "I'm thinking then I'd better get your room ready. You'll be using mine. And you, Mr. Carter, will have to make do in the catchall, I'm afraid. There's a cot in there along with a lot of stuff I've been meaning to throw out and some I don't know where to put. Unless you'd rather take the sofa in the front room. It's softer but"—he thoughtfully eyed Luke's big frame—"it might be kind of short."

"The cot'll do okay."

Samantha watched Luke watching Sol leave the room, certain that Luke was waiting for a chance to ask more questions. She struggled for composure.

Sol no sooner disappeared from view than Luke turned his attention to her. "How long are you staying in Ireland?" He swallowed some Scotch and eyed her over the rim of the glass.

It was a perfectly ordinary question, and his tone was quite casual. So why was her stomach jumping? "Oh, only a day or so."

He raised an eyebrow. "A few hours in Amsterdam, just a day or so in Ireland. You really move around, don't you."

She forced a smile. "I'm a model on a fashion-shooting assignment. How long I stay in a place depends on how quickly the job gets done."

"A model, are you? Yes, I can see why." He pointed a thumb at the storm-pelted window behind him. "I hope you're modeling rainwear. By the way, how was the weather in Amsterdam?"

She tried to steady her cup. "Amsterdam? Why . . . it was—it was nice."

"Interesting city, Amsterdam. Windmills. Tulips. And of course, diamonds."

Tea sloshed dangerously.

"You know," he went on, "you forget Amsterdam is a diamond center until you hear news like that guy getting knocked off. Let's see, what was his name?"

"They didn't give it," she said in a small voice.

"Oh, I've been hearing that broadcast all day on the car radio. Now, let me think. Von something? No, not Von. Oh, yes . . ."

She braced herself.

"Van something. Yes, that's it. VanDam."

Another teacup hit the hearth.

Luke got to his feet. "I'll get a towel." He stood a moment, looking down at her. "Want to change your mind about that Scotch?"

"Yes, please."

He returned with a towel and a glass, poured a generous portion of Scotch, and shoved it into her hands. Then he knelt and swiped the towel through the broken crockery and the puddle of tea. "Funny thing," he said in that chatty voice she was beginning to hate, "I wondered about that blonde they're looking for. The cabdriver said she was a knockout. Expensively dressed." He eyed her designer suit. "Why do you suppose a woman like that has to swipe diamonds?"

Samantha twisted the glass in her hands. "Why do the police say she swiped them?"

"There was something about an open safe and VanDam's body—" He broke off as Sol came through the doorway. He got to his feet and went over to the sink. "Had another little accident," he explained, getting rid of the dripping towel and the last bits of broken china.

"Oh?" Sol looked curiously at Samantha.

She was barely aware of him. Luke's words had just registered.

"Body?" she said faintly.

"Body?" Sol asked with interest.

"I think Miss Malloy's got a problem," Luke said.

31

" 'Body' being the key word?" Sol said.

"Right."

Samantha's mind whirled. Mijnheer VanDam dead? And the police looking for her? Why her? He had been alive when she left him. *Who's going to believe that?* a small inner voice asked. Her heart sank. No one else had been about at that early hour. Not even on the street. Except two men all muffled in scarves and wool caps who had been coiling hoses at the rear of a battered blue truck in front of Mijnheer VanDam's house. But they'd be poor witnesses. Not only had they not looked up when she got out of the cab, they hadn't looked up when she left. Not even when she dropped envelopes all over the doorstep as she struggled to close the door with her hands full of suitcase, handbag, and letters to be mailed. They just went on coiling hoses. Heads down. So neither would they have caught that brief glimpse of Mijnheer VanDam when he appeared at the window to wave a feeble hand at her. She felt Luke's and Sol's eyes on her and took a large gulp of Scotch. Immediately the fiery liquor hit her empty stomach and spread out in all directions. She ran a shaky hand across her forehead.

"And whose body is it that we're speaking of?" Sol asked.

"That guy in Amsterdam they've been broadcasting about all day. The quarter-million-dollar diamond robbery—"

Samantha sat bolt upright. "A quarter of a million dollars?" she asked, finding her voice. "But . . . that's —that's—" She caught herself. "I didn't hear the announcer say anything about a quarter of a million dollars worth of diamonds being stolen."

"Well, there were. The police found some kind of scribbled record of the guy's inventory."

"You certainly seem to know a lot about the matter," Samantha said, and took another swallow of Scotch. She had to grab on to the arms of the rocker until the room stopped spinning and bucking.

"Well, it was a long drive and I heard the broadcast a lot of. . . ." Luke's voice trailed off, and a thoughtful look came into his eyes.

Samantha looked away, trying to marshal her thoughts. Mustn't tell these fellows anything. Mustn't let the cat out of the bag. Warren wouldn't like that. No, indeed. Wouldn't like that at all. Besides it was a horrible mistake, the police wanting her. Why weren't they looking for the real criminals? She certainly didn't know anything about any quarter-million-dollar robbery. So why did Luke Carter say she had a problem? "Why do you say I have a problem? I don't have any problem. I certainly don't know anything about any quarter-million diamond dollary murder . . . I mean diamond-robbery murdery.

"So let's leave it at that, shall we?" Luke said firmly, as though he'd reached some conclusion.

"Sure, and Miss Malloy wasn't even in Amsterdam this morning, were you, Miss Malloy?" Sol said.

"Never mind," Luke said in a sharp voice.

Sol and Samantha both looked at him.

"Let's just drop the whole subject, shall we?" Luke said in a more normal tone.

"Oh?" Sol said.

"Oh?" said Samantha.

"When the police get on the trail of that blonde—and they will, you can bet on that—they're going to be rounding up anyone who's even looked cross-eyed at her. Now I've no time to be hanging around these parts answering questions if that blonde should happen to turn out to be Miss Malloy. No, no, don't say a word."

Luke waved a protesting hand as Samantha opened her mouth. "Not a word. When I leave here in the morning, the less I know, the better."

"Well!" It was one thing, Samantha felt, if she chose not to lay her cards on the table, but it was something else for Luke Carter not to give a damn whether or not she was being wrongfully accused of robbery and murder. She drained her drink in one swallow and set the glass down with a thud, her face reddening. "Now, that's just what's wrong with the world today!"

"What is that?" Sol asked, moving to the edge of his seat.

"You ask what is that?" She fumbled with the buttons of her jacket, the room suddenly too warm. "I'll tell you what is that. What is that is people like Mr. Carter here, not wanting to get involved in my problems. That's what is that." A glittering eye pinned Luke. "Anyway you're already mixed up in them. You and your questions! You know I was in Amsterdam—"

"Oh, Christ," Luke said.

"You were?" Sol said. "You were in Amsterdam?"

"I most certainly was in Amsterdam," she said. And then paused to consider. Yes, that's what she had said all right. *I most certainly was in Amsterdam.* Just like that. Spilled the beans. She had not had the stones twenty-four hours and the cat was out of the bag. Warren would be a basket case. She leveled in on Luke. "See what you made me do."

"Hold it. Don't go blaming me."

"Oh, izzat—" She stopped and started again. "Oh, is that so?" she carefully said. "You've done everything but accuse me outright of stealing and murdering—"

"Now just a minute," Luke said, looking uncomfortable.

"Just a minute, nothing," she said, warming to the

issue. "Let me tell you Mijnheer VanDam was perfectly all right when I left him, and the only reason I was there in the first place was to buy diamonds. Fifty thousand dollars worth. And that's what I did. Bought and paid for them." And that she could prove. She had the bill of sale. All carefully prepared by Warren and irritably completed by Mijnheer VanDam. "And I can prove it. But I can't prove he was alive when I left." She sat back, breathing heavily.

Luke reflected for a moment. Then he turned to Sol, sighing, "Well, I'd say she's mixed us up in this right proper."

"Right proper," Sol agreed. He leaned forward. "Fifty thousand dollars worth of diamonds, Miss Malloy?"

Instinctively she clutched her bosom.

"Oh, hell," Luke said, eyeing her hands with obvious disappointment.

She hastily dropped her hands. "Well, are you going to help me?"

"The best help I can give you is to advise you to get in touch with the nearest authorities and tell them what you just told us."

"I can't do that."

"Why not? I thought you said you could prove it. That you bought fifty thousand dollars worth of diamonds anyway."

"It'd get in all the papers, wouldn't it? Even the American ones?"

"So what, if you're innocent? I should think publicity would be right up a model's alley. Probably get you on talk shows."

It would also raise the question of where had she got the money to buy the diamonds. And the answer to that one would keep Warren busy answering the door and telephone for some time—if he didn't jump out the window first. "No, I don't want that kind of publicity. Besides by morning they'll probably have caught the real criminal anyway."

"Suit yourself," Luke said.

"You don't believe me, do you?" Tears welled.

Sol quickly patted her hand. "We believe you, Miss Malloy. Honest."

The tears spilled over. Sol was a kind person. "You're a kind person, Sol."

"Now don't. Don't you start crying," Luke said.

"You think I stole the diamonds—"

"No, no. If you say you bought them, you bought them. Just don't cry."

She sniffled. "I told you I bought them. Here, I'll prove it. I'll show you the bill of sale." She reached down for her handbag and almost toppled out of her chair. Both Luke and Sol grabbed her. The room swam. She steadied her head with her hands. "Oh, my!" she said as the room settled. She waved them off. " 'S all right. Juz dissy." She plopped the bag on her lap and wrestled with the zipper.

Luke and Sol exchanged glances.

" 'S right here," she said, pawing through her purse. She removed tissues and maps onto her lap. "Right here someplace." A small camera and a makeup kit came out. She frowned. A red silk coin purse, car keys, and several loose coins joined the heap.

Sol shifted his feet, and Luke began whistling under his breath.

"Where is the blasted thing?" She pulled out her passport and three folders of traveler's checks, her billfold, and some travel brochures from the airlines.

Luke and Sol exchanged glances again.

She pulled out a scarf, a pair of gloves, a roll of candy mints, a small tin of aspirin, and a currency-exchange folder. And then she frantically turned the bag upside down and shook it. Empty. In panic she pawed through the pile on her lap. There was no bill of sale.

She looked up, eyes wide with disbelief. "It's gone!"

CHAPTER IV

She sat staring dumbly at the empty handbag. For a moment no one spoke and the sounds of the storm filled the room. Rain beat down on the roof. Wind moaned along the eaves. Shutters rattled.

Then Luke stirred and cleared his throat. "You're . . . uh . . . you're sure you got a receipt, are you?"

She bristled. "What do you mean, am I sure? I ought to know whether I got a receipt or not, shouldn't I? It was in my purse when I left Cork. I saw it when I was settling with the car agent."

"Then it must've fallen out of your purse. It's probably on the seat or the floor of the car."

She sagged with relief. "Of course. That's where it is."

"I'll get it," Sol said, leaping to his feet.

"I'll go with you," she said, hastily stuffing things back into the handbag.

"Nice night for a swim," Luke said.

Samantha threw a glance at the dripping window. "I'll be at the front window," she told Sol, holding the car keys out to him.

Luke watched her follow Sol. The shock of the past few minutes had brought her eyes back into focus but her gait was a far cry from the glide of her entrance. He shook his head and for a moment or so sat with an eye and an ear cocked to the doorway. Then he sighed, pushed out of his chair, and went into the shadowy dimness of the front room, taking a place beside Samantha at the window. They watched Sol's flashlight play through the small car.

"Just to satisfy my curiosity," Luke said, "what in

hell are you doing running around with a chest full of diamonds?"

It was a good question. "I'm not surprised you asked that."

"Well?"

"It's—it's sort of involved."

"I had the feeling it was."

She felt her face flush and was glad the darkened room kept him from seeing it. Why did she suddenly feel Warren's idea wasn't the great thing it had seemed back in New York? There was nothing wrong with a man using his own money to make an investment or even concealing the fact from a partner. Especially when it was for special favors on the side. Just the same, something told her Luke wouldn't think much of the idea, and the way she felt at the moment she'd just as soon not have to defend it. "I'd rather not go into it," she told Luke.

"Suit yourself."

She found herself inexplicably annoyed with his willingness to let her go it alone, but before she could develop this theme, the car door slammed and she rushed to meet Sol. "You found it?"

"No," he said, shaking off the rain. "It wasn't anywhere in the car."

"Not anywhere! But it must be!"

"It isn't, Miss Malloy. I searched both the front and back seats."

"Then where could it be?"

"Where indeed?" Luke said.

She turned on him. "Where indeed, where indeed," she snapped. "You don't believe there is a bill of sale. Well, there is and it's got to be in the car. I'm going to look for myself—"

Sol put out a restraining hand. "I looked everywhere. Really I did. Maybe it blew away when you got out."

"I don't see how. I only got out once before—" She brought herself up short, suddenly remembering white things sailing off into the dark blustery Irish night. "Oh!"

"Oh?" Sol said.

"Ah!" Luke said.

"Oh, ah, is right," she said triumphantly to Luke. "If that bill of sale is gone, it's all your fault! When I had to get out to clean off the mud that you spattered on the windshield, that's when it blew away. With the tissues. The wind swooped down and blew a bunch of stuff out of my hands and over half the countryside." She jabbed a forefinger into his chest. "It's probably in the next county by now, and it's all your fault."

He took a step away from the prodding finger and rubbed his chest. "Stop saying it's my fault. In the first place you shouldn't have had an important document like that loose in your purse."

"It was perfectly safe until I had to get out in all that rain because you—"

"Okay, okay, don't go into that again. The thing's gone no matter who's at fault." He ran his hands through his hair.

Sol went over to the fire and began stirring the faintly glowing embers.

Samantha sank down on the leather couch. "So what do we do now?" She looked up at Luke.

"We? Don't give me that 'we' stuff. I'm just passing through."

"You mean you're not going to help me?"

He lowered himself into an armchair and fished out a crumpled package of cigarettes from his pocket. "Help you what? Beat the rap? Skip the country?"

"Why do you keep making me sound like a criminal? All I did was buy some diamonds."

40

"Then you'd better trot yourself to the nearest police station and tell that to the authorities." He lit his cigarette and tossed the match at the fireplace. "Whether you're innocent or not, you were on the scene and those birds in Amsterdam'll be wanting to question you. Take it from me, you'll look a hell of a lot more innocent if you've stepped forward rather than had to be hauled in."

"With no bill of sale to back up my innocence? Anyway, how would they find me? They don't know who I am, let alone where I am."

"Oh, they'll track you down all right. For one thing if you got a bill of sale—"

"You see?" she said to Sol. "He doesn't believe I got one."

Luke took a ragged breath. "What I meant to say was if you—ah—the copy of your bill of sale has certainly been found by now so the police know—"

"No, they don't."

"Why not?"

"Because Mijnheer VanDam didn't make a copy of the bill of sale."

"Nonsense. He must've. There's got to be a strict rule about diamond brokers—"

"Well, he wasn't actually a diamond broker. He just happened to have these diamonds and—ah, a friend of mine heard they were for sale and—and told me about them."

Luke took his time digesting this information. "I see," he said, looking over at Sol outlined against the fireplace and poised in the act of replacing the poker. "What do you make of that, Sol?"

Sol carefully set the poker against the wall. "Well," he began briskly. "Well. . . ." He cleared his throat. "Well. . . ."

41

"Me too," Luke said. "Tell you what, Miss Malloy. I've got another bit of advice for you. Get yourself the best goddamned attorney you can find on either side of the Atlantic."

"If you're trying to frighten me," she said, her voice rising, "you're doing a good job."

"I'd be shaking in my boots myself. Only I'd be doing it at a police station. Claiming insanity while I was at it." He flung the half-smoked cigarette at the fireplace. "Of all the phony setups I ever heard—"

"It was not phony," she said, but her voice lacked that certain ringing quality that comes with firm conviction. Now and again she had wondered about Warren's mysterious client and their after-dark meetings in out-of-the-way places that had resulted in Warren's coming up with "a man in Amsterdam who has some diamonds." But the one time she had hinted something might be fishy, Warren had appeared crushed. Didn't she trust him? Of course she did. "It was not a phony deal," she repeated. "Mijnheer VanDam had some stones to sell and I bought them. What's wrong with that?"

"It's just a feeling I get," Luke said. "Okay, so they won't find a copy of the receipt but they'll sure as hell find your check or traveler's check with your name on it."

"No, they won't."

"I might've known. You paid in cash, right?"

"No, I didn't. I paid by cashier's check. And it's on its way to Switzerland. I know because I put the deposit in the mailbox myself.

Luke looked at her for a long minute. Then he pushed himself out of the chair and rubbed his hands briskly together. "Well, I've got to get an early start in the morning. Sol, where's this catchall of yours?"

Sol roused himself from his contemplation of Samantha. "Door on your left."

Samantha jumped up and clutched Luke's arm. "But—but what about me?"

"Get yourself that attorney."

"But—"

"But nothing. This whole deal smells from start to finish. Just remember one thing though. Before you're through, you're going to wish to hell you had left some identification behind."

"Why?" she asked warily.

"Why?" Sol asked curiously.

"Because the police are going to track you down, don't kid yourself about that. You're not exactly the type to melt in a crowd, you know."

"But they can't. I wore dark glasses—"

Luke snorted. "A beard wouldn't have helped. Not with what you've got—even though it's not all you." His regretful eye lit briefly on her chest. "I'll bet they're rounding up witnesses right now to every move you made from the time you arrived at VanDam's to the time you set down in Ireland. And when they don't find any evidence of a legitimate reason for your being at that bird's place this morning, your chances of getting them to swallow that story you just handed us will disappear like smoke before the wind."

She sank back onto the sofa. "I never thought of that."

"Well, think about it."

Sol leaned toward her. "Was anyone around when you left? Anyone who saw the fellow still alive?"

She shook her head. "He didn't come to the door with me. He was an old man and all crippled with arthritis. I told him I'd let myself out and offered to post his letters for him so he wouldn't have to go out in the cold."

43

"And you're sure, are you, that your check was in one of them?" Sol said.

"He got it ready for deposit in front of me and gave me the envelope along with two others. I dropped them all getting out the front door, and when I picked them up off the steps, I noticed all three were addressed to Swiss banks."

"That figures," Luke said with disgust. He stood looking down at her for a moment, then said, "This cashier's check you gave him, was it made out to him personally?"

"Yes."

"Then there's no problem. All you have to do is get the police to contact your bank."

"That wouldn't help," she said in a faint voice, bracing for Luke's blast.

"Oh, Jesus!"

"Now what?" Sol said.

Warren had bought the check of course, warning her that if it were ever traced back to him it would be good-bye Councilman Beck or Alderman Beck or whatever it was he had his eye on. He had given her the idea that in such an event her wedding bells would land on the same heap as his smashed ambitions. She drew herself in. "It . . . a friend bought the check." She sighed.

Luke sighed.

Sol sighed.

"He . . . I . . . my friend's name must not be connected with this business in any way."

In the brief silence that fell she could feel Luke's penetrating eyes and once more was grateful the darkened room spared her.

Then abruptly Luke shifted his focus to Sol. "Door on the left, you said?" He picked up his muddy bags.

"You're going to bed," she said with sad acceptance of one more real toad in her imaginary garden.

44

"That's right, Miss Malloy. I'm going to bed. I'm just an engineer, you know. Any time you want a road or a dam or a bridge built, give me a call. But when it comes to grappling with hot diamonds and cold bodies, I'm with your mysterious friend. Count me out too." He loomed over her. "Just remember—" He broke off as headlights flashed into the room.

The three of them remained fixed while a car drew up. The room darkened, and the next moment a car door slammed.

Sol sprang to the closest window.

"Oy vay," he keened, "the fuzz!"

CHAPTER V

"Oh, my God!" Samantha cried. Luke grabbed her by the arm and pulled her into the deeper shadows of the room as Sol moved to answer the peremptory bang on the door.

"Evening, Mr. Donegal," Sol said, his manner formal. "Will you be coming in?"

"Evening, Solomon. I will that, thank you." Mr. Donegal stepped across the threshold and into the firelight. He was a round, rosy-faced little man splendidly dressed all in black, with well-laced shoes polished to the inch and a straight-brimmed hat sitting squarely on his white-thatched head. He brushed raindrops off his sleeves. " 'Tis a filthy night out," he said, his manner as formal as Sol's.

" 'Tis that," Sol agreed.

Mr. Donegal's bright blue eyes darted about the room and landed on Luke and Samantha. He nodded. "Good evening."

"Good evening," Luke said, and then jabbed an elbow into Samantha's ribs.

"Oh . . . good evening," she said, rallying.

"Mr. Donegal is our equivalent of your chief of police back home," Sol explained. "He lives a few villages away and has charge of all this area." For a brief moment Sol stood irresolute. Then, as though a button had been pressed, he moved swiftly to the fireplace and got busy with poker and embers and a fresh cake of peat. "Mr. Donegal's first granchild was baptized here today. A fine grandson," he went on.

Samantha and Luke murmured "Oh" and "Ah," and Sol continued smoothly, "And these, Mr. Donegal, are . . . His jabbing and poking at the grate drowned out his voice for a moment. " . . . and Luke Carter, my friends from the States," he wound up, setting the poker aside with an air of accomplishment.

"I'd not heard you were expecting company from home," Mr. Donegal said, as though someone had been remiss.

"It was an unexpected visit," Luke said quickly. "Just passing through, you know."

"Ah," said Mr. Donegal, pacified. "And the fine car in the ditch is yours, I'm thinking?"

"Yes, it is."

"I'm hoping neither you nor Mrs. Carter was hurt."

Luke gave an involuntary start, and Samantha could feel his eyes on her. Mrs. Carter? Deliverance? With an eye to the main chance she snatched at the opportunity. "No, no. We weren't hurt." Luke made a small explosive sound, and she held her breath. He let the moment pass.

"I'm glad," Mr. Donegal said and turned to Sol. "Well now, 'twas only that I spied the car on my way home and thought it best that I investigate. I'll just be getting along now." He made no move to go, however, but remained, looking at Sol. " 'Tis a wet drive that's ahead of me," he said, fixing Sol with a glinty eye.

"Ah, yes," Sol said quickly. "Then will you be having a bit of drink to warm your way?"

Samantha could have hit him. A close look at her under the kitchen light could be but a step away from the click of handcuffs. Still and all, she half-expected Mr. Donegal to refuse. There seemed to be an undercurrent of shoving and pushing held in control that didn't lend itself to the sharing of a friendly sip.

"Thank you, Solomon, I will that."

So much for perception. She gave Luke a "Do-something" poke. He returned the hot eye of "Like-what?" She had no idea what to do, but these could be her last free moments. She gave him another poke.

"If you don't mind, Sol," Luke said, rubbing his rib and moving a step away, "I think we'll turn in. It's been a long day."

"Come a way, have you?" Mr. Donegal asked, his gaze resting on Samantha.

"From Cork," she said, rattled.

"London," Luke said firmly. "Cork was where we had dinner," he told Mr. Donegal. "She only counts from the last stop." He picked up his bags and Samantha's small case. "Your room, you said, Sol?"

"Yes, the door on the right. The bathroom's just beyond."

They had taken no more than a couple of steps when Mr. Donegal said briskly, "Now would you be waiting, please?"

Samantha froze. She waited for the dreaded words.

"I'm thinking, Mr. Carter, you'd do well not to leave anything of value in your car. Or even in the boot. There's tinkers up at the fork. If it were my car, I'd be making that much of an effort to move it out of the ditch and into Solomon's garage as long as he's daft enough to leave his out on the road."

Samantha let out her breath.

"It won't budge without help," Luke said. "Sol's going to arrange some first thing in the morning."

"Anyway it's not likely tinkers would be out in this weather," Sol said.

"It's little you know of tinkers, then," Mr. Donegal said. "The weather'll not be keeping them from stealing anything they can lay their thieving hands on."

"Well, there's nothing of value in the car," Luke assured him. Then he nudged Samantha. "Come along, my dear," he said heavily.

She followed him the few steps along the short pas-

48

sageway to the door opposite the kitchen. Once inside she leaned against the wall, trying to control her jangling nerves. She looked around the small neat room, which was decorated in the same bright yellows, reds, and blues as the kitchen. There were small braided rugs on the polished floor and a huge eiderdown on the bed. A guitar stood in a corner and a covered easel against a wall. Several oils and watercolors, all done with a lively sense of color and style, hung unframed about the room.

Sol had left a lamp burning low on the nightstand. Luke turned it up and then opened his suitcase on the bed. He rummaged inside, pulled out pajamas, tossed them on the bed, and delved deeper into the suitcase.

Samantha felt life had become complicated enough. "You can get that idea out of your head," she said firmly.

"What?" he muttered, busy in the depths of the bag. "Ah, here we are!" He brought forth a fat squat bottle. "What did you say?"

"You're wasting your time."

He followed her eyes to his pajamas. "I see. No dice?"

"No dice."

He shrugged lightly. "Pity." Then he held up the bottle. "Care to join me?"

"I've had enough," she said, illogically annoyed with him.

"Oh, come on, it'll relax you. What's a little more weaving and slurring among partners in crime?"

Weaving and slurring were not the words usually associated with her. She drew herself up haughtily. "No thank you, Mr. Carter, I'm—" A tap at the door cut her off. It was Sol. "Has he gone?" she asked, coming off her high horse.

"He has."

49

"Did he say anything? About, you know, my looking like anyone they're after?" Her expression beseeched him to say no.

He was happy to oblige. "I'm that certain he doesn't even know they're after anyone. He's been celebrating the baptism all day and couldn't care less what's going on in the criminal world. Lucky your car is the same model as mine, though. I forgot about it being out on the road. It would have been hard explaining why you were traveling in two cars. Even Americans aren't that crazy." He eyed Luke's bottle. "Armagnac?"

Luke offered the bottle, and when Sol had taken a swig and handed it back, he rubbed his hands briskly. "Well, now, and where were we before we were interrupted?"

"In a hell of a lot less trouble than we are now," Luke said.

"And why is that?"

"You and I, me boyo, are now accessories after the fact." The look he gave Samantha fixed the blame.

She stiffened. "That's not true. There's no fact for you to be accessory after. How many times do I have to tell you I bought those diamonds?"

"You don't have to tell me. Tell the police. And may I say you missed an excellent opportunity to make a— excuse the expression—clean breast of it to Mr. Donegal."

"How could I without giving the lie to Sol's introducing me as Mrs. Carter?" She could think on her feet when she had to. But Luke wasn't buying it.

"That's not quite the way it was. There was a moment there when you could have set things straight and we all could have had a good laugh and then you could have gone on to tell your little story."

"I've told you I can't go to the police. Someone else is involved and the publicity would ruin him. Anyway I just know it'll all be straightened out tomorrow." She sighed. "In any case I'll be leaving first thing in the morning, and nobody'll ever know you even heard of me."

Luke regarded her briefly and then gathered up his gear. "Okay, then, good luck, Miss Malloy. Come on, Sol, let's have a nightcap."

"There are towels in the bathroom," Sol said. "And there's a shower but I'm not sure there's hot water—the electricity being out, you see." He paused in the doorway. "I'm sure everything'll turn out all right, Miss Malloy."

She found it hard to return his smile, and when the door closed behind him, she felt abandoned by the world.

She trudged through the preparations for bed. The water was not hot and the bathroom was freezing cold. She skimped on the ritual of creams and oils, skipped rolling up her hair, gave a moment's thought to sleeping in her diamond-laden bra, decided to hell with them, and was shivering her way back to the bedroom when headlights once more flashed into the darkened living room. She stopped dead in her tracks.

"And now what?" she heard Sol say. There was the sound of moving about and then both men were outlined in the fire's glow against the window.

"Christ," Luke said. "Mr. Donegal again."

"The very same," Sol said bleakly.

CHAPTER VI

Luke grabbed his gear and legged it down the hall and into the immobile Samantha. "Come on, we're supposed to have gone to bed," he said, prodding her to life and into the bedroom as Mr. Donegal began rapping at the door.

Once inside they stood transfixed, listening to the mumble of voices and the sounds of bustling siphoning through the thick walls. After what seemed an eternity to Samantha, there was a tapping at the bedroom door and Sol called out with forced brightness, "I've got your extra blankets, Luke."

Luke opened the door and Sol stepped in, blankets over his arm. With a cautioning jerk of the head he said in the same loud voice, "Here you are. These should keep you warm. Oh, by the way, Mr. Donegal's returned. The bridges are under water and he can't get out of Riverford. He doesn't want to wake the new mother and baby so he's spending the night with us." His grimace shunted the blame for this state of affairs.

"Is that so?" Luke said, also in a carrying voice.

"Yes," Sol said, pausing significantly. "He's going to sleep on the couch in front of the fire."

"I see," Luke said. Then a look of dawning awareness spread over his face, and immediately he had trouble controlling a grin as he glanced over to Samantha. "He's going to sleep on the couch," he said.

"In the front room," Sol added with emphasis.

Samantha readily saw the problem involved, but she was confident she could handle it. "That's nice," she said when it appeared a comment was expected.

"Well," said Luke, directing his voice through the

open doorway, "thanks for the blankets. See you in the morning."

"Good night," Sol said, backing out of the room. "Sleep, you know, well."

Luke closed the door and, still grinning, dumped the blankets on a chair, then sat down on the edge of the bed. "Well, well, well. Looks like we're roommates," he said, unlacing his shoes.

"It's an awkward situation, but I suppose we can work something out," she said, her mind searching out the possibilities.

"Oh, I'm sure of it," he said cheerfully. He kicked off his shoes and, rising, began unbuttoning his shirt.

She came out of her preoccupation with a jerk. "What do you think you're doing?"

"Getting ready for bed. I see you already are." He peeled off his shirt and started unbuckling his belt.

"You can stop right there," Samantha ordered.

He stopped and gave her a blank look. "What the hell? You think I'm going to sleep in my trousers?"

"You can sleep however you want to. But not in here," she said in the manner of a duchess laying down the ground rules to a fractious peasant.

"And where would you suggest I sleep?"

The answer was simple, and she wondered why she hadn't thought of it immediately. "You can go in with Sol as soon as Mr. Donegal's asleep."

"And, I suppose, sneak back in the morning before he wakes up?" he asked.

His cold eye and the edge to his voice hinted she might not be in as total control of the situation as she might wish. Nonetheless she returned his stony gaze and said, "Exactly."

"That's what you think," he said, confirming her suspicions. "What the hell do you think this is? A Marx Brothers' movie? I'm not tiptoeing in and out of bedrooms all night, I'll tell you right now." He unbuckled his belt. "If you don't like this arrangement, just trot on out to Mr. Donegal and lay your cards on the table. Which would probably be the smartest thing you've done all day."

"That's out of the question."

"In that case. . . ." His hands went to his zipper and paused. His lips twitched. "Ready or not . . . " he said, ill-concealing the underlying laughter.

She turned her back on him. Her anger rose. Her rather grand self-image had taken a beating these past few hours, and being laughed at was the capper. "You're not making a difficult situation any easier," she snapped.

"You're the one who created the situation."

She chose not to dwell on that. "You could at least undress in the bathroom."

"Donegal might find that strange, don't you think? You letting him believe we're married and all."

"Do you have to keep harping on that?"

"I just want to keep the record straight."

"Anyway, Donegal's probably in the kitchen drinking with Sol," she said bitterly. No one had the right to enjoy himself when her world was crumbling under her feet.

"Probably."

"Then would you mind undressing in the bathroom?"

"Too late. I'm a fast undresser. You can turn around now," he said above the sounds of repacking and stowing away of gear.

She ignored the invitation. "You're an insensitive— insensitive—" She floundered among the possibilities.

"Cad?" he said.

"Bully."

"Ah!" he exclaimed, as if approving of her choice.

Then, changing his tone, he said, "Tell me, are your delicate sensibilities offended because a man undressed in the same room with you or because I was the man?"

Of course it had not been a question of outraged virtue. All things considered, such a stand would have been absurd. But, she told herself, it was his take-it-or-leave-it attitude, his not even asking if she'd mind. So a small voice within her asked, if he had asked, what then? Well, then, the circumstances being what they were, she would've given permission. It was simply the principle involved. And it would have put their relationship on an easier basis and made things pleasanter. And then what? She considered the question and found herself thinking of the breadth of his shoulders, the line of his jaw. She imagined tracing a finger along it, and brought herself up with a start. What nonsense was this? Realizing that she hadn't answered his question, she said curtly, "That is one of those trick questions, and I have no intention of answering it."

He chuckled. "It doesn't matter. I know the answer anyway."

She bit her tongue to keep from asking what he thought the answer was and instead concentrated on the problem at hand. Looking about the room, she came up with the solution. "Very well, if you insist on staying in here," she said, "you can put chairs together in some sort of bed for yourself."

"Guess again, Miss Malloy."

She turned to find him stretching out beneath the covers. "Now look here, Mr. Carter—"

"No, you look here, Miss Malloy," he said, rising on an elbow and fixing her with a level eye. "I've been traveling since dawn and I'm tired. I've got to jockey a car out of a ditch in the morning and then put in a full day getting a bid together. And just as soon as that's done, I've got to turn around and drive the car back to its owner in London before I catch a plane back to a job halfway around the world, where we're working around the clock against a deadline." He turned and punched the pillow into a more pleasing shape. "Now, I'm going to get one night's decent sleep in this nice soft bed, and if you don't want to share it, that's your tough luck."

She stared at him, stunned. "I can't believe you're serious," she said.

"Believe it," he said with disheartening firmness. Then he grinned. "Come on. I'll stay on my side and you stay on your side."

"I'll do no such thing," she snapped.

"Great!"

"And that's not what I meant."

"Rats."

She stood there wanting to yell and throw things but she was certain that would only amuse him. Besides, the racket would give Mr. Donegal enough food for thought to keep him awake the rest of the night.

She marched over to the bed and snatched up the eiderdown and a pillow.

"Sleep well," he said pleasantly, turning on his side and burrowing into his own pillow.

She glared at him in stony silence for a moment, then turned on her heel and angrily dragged two chairs as far away from the bed as possible. Wrapping the quilt around her, she tried to settle herself on the makeshift bed. First thing in the morning she'd stop in the village and put in a call to Warren before going on to Parknasilla. That's what she should have done when she heard that newscast. He probably could've straightened this mess out in nothing flat and she wouldn't be in this ridiculous situation. She yanked the quilt tighter and the chairs slid apart, scraping loudly along the polished floor. She sat up, jerked them back together, and re-arranged the quilt around her.

"Comfy?" Luke's voice came across the darkness.

"What do you think?" she said grimly.

"I think you're being stupid. Come on. I promise I won't lay a hand on you. Scout's honor."

"You don't strike me as Scout material," she said frigidly. The effect was marred, however, for once more the chairs slid apart and she had to scramble to keep from sitting on the floor. It was clear what kind of a night this was going to be. She'd be in fine shape to face the cameras in the morning—a problem she'd overlooked in the rush of events. And this was a problem she could relate to, one that threatened the world she lived in as opposed to some fanciful one filled with accusations of mayhem and thievery. The other three models on the trip would just love to have her show up drawn and hollow-eyed, to be banished to the sidelines. She shook her head in despair. A mistake. Wearily she got to her feet again to rearrange the chairs. Perhaps they wouldn't slide around so much on the braided rugs. She prepared to drag them across the wooden floor and found herself scooped off her feet.

"What—what do you think you're doing!" she sputtered.

"Oh, shut up," Luke ordered. "If you think I'm going to spend the night listening to you fall out of those damned chairs, you're crazy." He dumped her onto the bed and threw the eiderdown over her. "Now," he said in a no-nonsense voice, "I don't want to hear a peep out of you. You stay on your side of the bed and I'll stay on mine, so for Christ's sake relax and go to sleep."

She felt the bed heave and billow as he got under the covers and thumped about for a comfortable position. The arrangement was a vast improvement over the chairs, and she decided not to let principle cut off the nose of common sense. Just the same she felt compelled to register some protest. "I don't know what Warren'll say about this," she said with as much dignity as she could muster under the circumstances.

"Son of a bitch, probably," Luke mumbled.

Not likely, she thought. Warren was given more to five-thousand-word lectures. She yawned, comfortable and warm. Outside the storm was still in full swing. Rain lashed at the windows, wind howled around corners. Her eyes grew heavy and closed.

"This Warren . . . your fiancé?"

"Yes," she said through the veil of sleep.

After a moment's silence Luke said, "He's the guy you're trying to keep in the clear, of course."

"Yes." She roused briefly to think about that. Should she have admitted it? She shrugged. To hell with it. At the moment she wasn't all that crazy about Warren or his blasted ideas.

Luke grunted and burrowed into his pillow.

The rain had stopped during the night. At least, hanging on to the remnants of sleep, Luke couldn't hear any hitting the window. What he did hear was a soft rustling and pattering. He listened a moment and then realized it was his roommate creeping about. He struck a match and found her getting into her coat.

Samantha looked around for her scarf. She was in a hurry to get started and had no time to lock horns with him this morning. Besides, she found herself thinking, it would be nice to leave him wishing things might have been different too. Too? The unbidden thought startled her. Why would she wish things had been different? She had Warren, didn't she? Of course she did. And she loved him. Didn't she? Of course she did. She hastily snatched up her scarf and turned away as he put the match to the lamp.

"It's not even five o'clock for God's sake," he said, trying to focus on his watch, his voice thick with sleep.

"I know." It was early, even for a model whose day usually began on the dreary side of 6:00 A.M. That careless, natural look takes a lot of time.

"Think you'll get past Mr. Donegal?"

"He's sound asleep. Snoring. I checked." She gave the scarf a final tug and turned back to him, eyeing him uncertainly. "You . . . it'll be awkward, won't it, explaining my absence. . . ."

His expression was calm. "Don't give it a thought. I'll think of something."

"Well . . . well. . . ." She took a deep breath and, mustering some semblance of the old assurance, went over to the bed and held out her hand. "Good-bye, Mr. Carter."

He took her hand, eyeing her bosom. "I see you've got the loot back in the old safe."

"Yes . . . well . . . good-bye." She tugged her hand free. "It was nice. . . ." Her voice trailed off. Why was she dragging this out? She turned abruptly and made for the door.

"Good luck, Miss Malloy," he said softly as she slipped out. For a moment he gazed thoughtfully at the door and then lay back, arms behind his head. He turned to look at the still-indented pillow beside his and shook his head, regretting his continence of the night before. "Oh, hell," he said and turned away to reach for the switch on the lamp. The door burst open. Samantha was back.

She shut the door quickly and fell against it, white-faced and strained. "My tires are gone!" she wailed.

He shot up. "Gone?"

"All four of them." She moved into the room.

"What the hell—" Then he snapped his fingers. "The tinkers! Mr. Donegal said they— Oh, my God! My car!" He leaped out of bed, yanked his trousers on over his pajamas, and jammed his feet into his shoes. "You don't suppose those bastards—" He grabbed his jacket and was out the door before she could close her mouth.

She was still standing in the middle of the room when Sol shuffled up to the open doorway. "What's going on?" he whispered over the loud snoring in the front room.

She pulled him inside and shut the door. "My tires are gone. Somebody stole my tires. All four of them."

"*Oy!*" He slapped his forehead. "The tinkers!"

"What am I going to do? I have to get to Parknasilla."

"I . . . let me think." He looked around helplessly. "Where's Mr. Carter?"

"He went to check his car. Do you suppose they got his tires too?"

"Seems likely."

"Oh, what am I going to do?" She sagged. "I've got to—I know! Mr. Donegal's car. I'll—" She stopped short. "Sol, Mr. Donegal's car wasn't out in front. Could they have stolen—"

"No, no. He put it in my garage, thinking your car was mine and, as he said, seeing that I was daft enough to leave it out."

"I just hope the keys are in it," she said, starting for the door.

"Miss Malloy, wait!"

"I'll leave a note," she said desperately. "Or maybe he'll think the tinkers—" She saw he was shaking his head. "Sol, I've *got* to get to Parknasilla."

"The bridges, Miss Malloy. Are you forgetting they're underwater?"

"But it stopped raining during the night."

"I know, but, well, those bridges are awfully old. They sag even in dry weather. And with the rivers rising in the storm. . . ."

She sank onto the nearest chair. "Isn't there any other way to get out of town?"

"There's a cart track across the hills back beyond the village, but it'd be too muddy for a car, I'm afraid." He sat on the edge of the bed, hunched over, his eyes sympathetic.

She roused herself. "Well, I'd better hike to the village and telephone to—" She assessed the expression on Sol's face. "Don't tell me, let me guess. There are no telephones in Riverford."

"No, that's not it. There's one in O'Callaghan's Emporium—that's Mr. Donegal's son-in-law, Hugh O'Callaghan. Only"—he squirmed—"nothing opens until around nine . . . sometimes."

"Sometimes?"

"Sometimes nothing opens until around ten or so. People around here don't pay too much attention to clocks."

She slumped back again. Sol sat yawning, scratching, and looking thoroughly distressed.

Then the door burst open and the room was full of Luke flinging his arms around and making the air blue with a summation of Ireland that would have wrung admiration from a Marine sergeant. He stopped only when he'd run out of breath.

"All four?" Sol said.

"No, two," Luke snapped. "But only because the other two were mired in the ditch."

"It doesn't matter much anyway," Samantha said

wearily. "The bridges are washed out and we're stuck in Riverford all day, it seems."

Sol cleared his throat. "Sometimes—sometimes those bridges are underwater for a couple of days." He swallowed. "And sometimes, after a big storm . . . like—like yesterday's . . . I understand they've been underwater for a week."

CHAPTER VII

Breakfast was a glum affair. The men put eggs into their mouths. Samantha stirred her coffee and passed the jam.

Mr. Donegal had long gone to his daughter's house, none too happy at having been awakened by Luke and Sol simply to be told of the thievery during the night. He reminded them with smug satisfaction, " 'Tis no more than I said would happen. Asking for trouble you were, leaving a car under the very noses of the tinkers."

No one pointed out that his own car had been spared by their seeming neglect. As for Luke's misfortune, the import of Mr. Donegal's "Ah, well . . ." consigned it to the hands of providence. He had given Luke a closer look, as though speculating upon what sins had earned such disfavor.

"You'd think," Luke said, shoving his plate aside, "the old bastard'd at least have made some notes or said something about filling out a report. Anything that would give the idea something was going to be done sometime or other."

Samantha couldn't agree more. Mr. Donegal's walking around the little hired car, shaking his head and clicking his tongue and then saying he'd have a look at Luke's car on the way past, wasn't her idea of proper police procedure. And yet, wouldn't such haphazard treatment of crime work be in her favor if the Amsterdam business got sticky? Her spirits lifted slightly.

"He'll get around to doing something," Sol said. "Nothing gets done in Ireland simply because it's time to do it. And if you don't mind, Mr. Carter, not 'old bastard,' please. 'Old goat,' if you will, but not 'old bastard.' You're speaking of the father of Mary, the joy of my heart, and the prettiest colleen in all of Ireland."

Samantha straightened, surprised. "Mr. Donegal's daughter?"

Luke's eyebrows climbed. "Donegal's daughter?"

Sol grinned. "She and her sister, Dierdre, favor their late mother, I'm told. You should see her," he said dreamily. "She's really something."

"I meant," Luke said, "if she's Donegal's daughter, you've got a problem."

"You noticed. However, now that I'm reopening O'Sullivan House, he's at least stopped spitting when I pass. Everyone expects it'll bring in tourist money and create jobs for Riverford."

Luke sat back and folded his arms. "Riverford had better get itself in line with the twentieth century then, before the twenty-first is here. And they might start by building some new bridges and tearing that damned tree out of the middle of the road. Otherwise the first jobs you'll have to create will be doctors and car mechanics to take care of the tourists piling up in the ditches."

Samantha nodded in agreement, remembering how she'd thought it odd to loop the road around the tree instead of removing it. She said as much to Sol.

"Ah, the tree." Sol shook his head. "That tree is a Fairy Thorn—a hawthorn that the Irish believe the fairies live in. No Irishman in his right mind would dream of disturbing it. The Little People would turn on him."

Ancestral memory stirred, and Mary Samantha Malooly surfaced. "The Little People . . ." she said, brightening.

"Aye, the fairies. They wield a lot of influence in these parts."

Luke snorted. "That figures."

"Don't scoff. One stood in the middle of a grading

site for one of those foreign outfits on the coast, and none of the Irish workers would have anything to do with removing it. The outfit's superintendent finally had to climb aboard the bulldozer, or whatever, and root it out himself. Fell and broke his leg getting down off the machine."

"Ah-ha!" said the last of the Maloolys.

"Oh, my God," said Luke.

"Say what you will," said Sol, "but you'll not be getting anyone in Riverford to touch that tree."

"I'll be damned if I don't think you believe in fairies yourself."

"No such thing," Sol said. Then he grinned. "But, as the old woman said, they're there."

Luke threw up his arms. "Fairies! Tinkers! My God, I don't believe this country!"

"Stick around," Sol said. "It'll get to you."

"That'll be the day." He crumpled his napkin and fished for a cigarette.

Samantha glanced at her watch. What with one thing and another they had missed the early-morning newscast, and the transistor played softly in the background while they waited for the next one. Her emotions were mixed. She looked forward to the broadcast, hoping the real criminal had been caught during the night, but on the other hand she dreaded it, fearing the net was closing in.

Luke lit his cigarette and threw the match into the fireplace. He too looked at the time, then said to her, "This outfit of yours, would they be likely to send out alarms when you don't show up? Two missing women with matching descriptions would have Amsterdam sitting up and taking notice."

The possibility was worth a fleeting-moment's worry but then Samantha dismissed it. It wasn't likely. The assumption would be that she had missed connections somewhere along the way, and the shooting would go ahead without her. She gloomily reviewed her position. Models who failed to keep assignments were dropped like hot potatoes. And she needed the work. She spent money as fast as she got it and had no reserve to fall back on while waiting for Warren to get around to putting the ring on her finger. "No," she said unhappily, "they'll just wash their hands of me and get on with the work."

"They'll probably shock hell out of the natives. Work seems to be a dirty word in Ireland. Sol, what're the chances of getting this O'Callaghan bird off his duff and opening up his shop? I've got a mess of figures I've got to get to my men before they work up a bid with the ones they've got. I stand to lose a hell of a wad of money if we get the job based on the costs they're using."

"And I could at least call Parknasilla and let them know I'm near," Samantha said, seeing a chance of saving her career.

Sol thought poorly of the idea. Mr. Donegal's presence at the O'Callahans' influenced his thought. "Your wanting to be in Parknasilla and Luke wanting to be on the coast might spark some questions you'd have trouble answering. Don't fool yourself. He's a sharp old bas—ah, a sharp one. And he may have heard the all-points bulletin from his headquarters on the two-way radio in his car, you know."

Samantha resigned herself to the unemployment line. Luke, however, saw no reason why his having business on the coast would trigger problems.

"You're right, of course," Sol said. "It's just that I'm thinking it a certainty that Mr. Donegal's gone back to bed at Dierdre's, and waking the whole house up is not something I'd look forward to."

"Is that all people do around here? Sleep?" Luke crushed out his cigarette. "Bridges or no bridges, I'm not sticking around here. I'd go nuts with nothing to do."

"Oh, there's a lot to do, and what's more, it gets done. But without being pushed by a clock."

"Or a calendar, I'll bet," Luke said, drumming his fingers on the table.

Samantha checked her watch again. It was time for the news. She didn't know which was worse—hearing it or worrying about it. "The eight o'clock news should be on," she said and felt her stomach tighten as Sol turned up the sound.

After bringing the latest catastrophes to his listeners' breakfast tables, the newscaster got to the Amsterdam affair. It was more detailed than the previous night's summary and when the estimated value of the stolen gems—two hundred fifty thousand dollars—was announced, Luke gave Samantha an I-told-you-so look and she gave an anguished moan. It was bad enough being wanted for fifty thousand dollars worth of diamonds that she'd bought. Being wanted for two hundred fifty thousand dollars worth that she knew nothing about was enough to smite the stoutest heart. Her despair mounted as the smooth voice concluded, "However, authorities are confident they've identified the young Canadian woman and will soon have her movements traced."

Luke turned the radio off, and Samantha paced about the room. "Why me? Why do they suspect me?"

"Probably because the cabdriver placed you at the scene of the crime at the time of the crime," Luke said.

Samantha felt his tone could have used more sympathy and less logic.

"You'd think that would tip them off that she's not

67

guilty," Sol said. "No criminal takes a cab to his victim's place, let alone fills the driver in on his background."

"There's always unpremeditated murder," Luke pointed out.

"I was there only about half an hour. How could I have opened a safe, ransacked a room, and murdered a man in that short time?"

"You could have had an accomplice planted earlier," Luke said. He waved her off as she angrily turned on him. "I'm not saying that's what happened. I'm only saying what the police might think."

"Well, it's ridiculous. Those cleaning men could've told them no one else arrived."

"Cleaning men?" Sol said.

"What cleaning men?" Luke asked sharply.

"There were two cleaning men in an old blue truck out in front of Mijnheer VanDam's house."

"But you said no one saw you," Luke said, his voice rising.

"Well, they didn't really. They barely looked up when I got out of the taxi. But they were coiling up hoses so they must've been there for some time. They would've noticed if anyone had arrived earlier. And what's more, they were still there winding up those hoses when I left. So they'd know no one was with me, even though they didn't actually look up."

Luke frowned. "They were still there? Still coiling hoses half an hour later?"

"Yes, so if there had been. . . . " Her voice trailed off as she imagined the scene. "That's funny. All those hoses, and nothing was wet. The walks and steps were dry."

"Are you sure?" Luke asked.

"Positive. Otherwise when I dropped Mijnheer Van-

Dam's letters, they'd have at least gotten damp. But when I picked them up and checked them, they were bone dry." She came back to the table and sat down. "Is that important?"

"I don't know," Luke said thoughtfully. "They could have been taking time out to straighten up their gear."

"Seems strange, though," Sol said. "No sign of water at all. And in the cool of early morning."

The doorknocker banged, jerking them to attention. In the next moment they heard the door open and a clear voice call, "Sol?"

Sol leaped to his feet, a smile lighting his face. "Mary! In here, Mary."

A small girl with a ribbon in her black curly hair appeared, flushed, in the doorway. She glanced swiftly at each of the faces in the kitchen, then, visibly relaxing, shifted her hold on a napkin-covered basket and moved purposefully into the room. Sol sprang to her side.

"This is Mary Donegal," he said, as though it were the signal for applause. "And this is"—he swallowed—"uh—"

"I know, Mr. and Mrs. Carter," Mary said, setting the basket down firmly on the table. "Father has told me." Her smile was quick and her eyes curious.

Luke stuck out his hand. "Hello, Mary. I'm Luke and this is Samantha."

Samantha nodded weakly, not at all happy about widening her circle of Donegals.

"Mary's taken leave from her job in London to be with her sister. The new baby, you know. And she's helped me fix up this place too," Sol said, and seemed to wait expectantly for the huzzahs.

"Oh?" Luke said politely.

"Oh?" Samantha said politely.

Mary took it all in stride and set about removing the snow-white napkin from the basket. "When Father told me Sol had unexpected company, I was thinking it was a sorry cupboard he keeps so I'll just be taking over some fresh bread and some newly made butter and a jar of Dierdre's jam," she said, bringing forth each item. "It's a poor welcome you've had from Ireland with the tinkers." She paused, frowning, then turned to Sol. "It's just come to me. Father said the tinkers carried off your tires too. But that cannot be your car on the road. Your car is in garage at Killarney."

"It's . . ." Sol floundered. He looked to Samantha.

"It's . . ." Samantha began. She looked to Luke.

"It's Samantha's," Luke said. "And that's a long story and right now I've got to get to a phone. As long as everyone's up at your sister's, will you take me over to—"

"But it won't do you any good," Mary said, a restraining hand on his arm as he shoved away from the table. "The wires are down. Father tried to call. The storm, you know."

Samantha groaned and Luke banged the table and said things behind his teeth that made Sol bite his lip and Mary roll her eyes. Then he got to his feet. "How soon before the wires are repaired?" he demanded, trying to shake off Mary's hold.

"But I've no idea," Mary said, renewing her grip. "Do be sitting down. There's nothing that a cup of tea—"

"I don't want any tea. I want a phone." Luke pried himself loose. "Now what's being done about getting those wires back up?"

Undaunted, Mary took his arm again. "When the bridges are passable, the repairmen will come and restore service."

Though Samantha was getting the hang of the Irish

and she could guess what Mary's answer would be, nevertheless she asked, "And how soon will that be, do you think?"

"Oh, sooner or later," Mary said, cheerfulness carefully sprinkled over her words.

"I knew she'd say that," Luke told Samantha.

"Me too," Samantha said morosely. She could hear the doors slamming on her career.

Sol softly cleared his throat. "People around here would rather visit over a cup of tea than on the telephone."

Luke's look told him what he could do with his cozy picture of Irish life.

"Now, then," Mary said brightly, "there's nothing that won't go down easier for a cup a cup of tea." A firm hand urged Luke down onto his chair.

"Oh, hell," Luke said, and sat.

Mary's pleased look took all of them in. "So, I'll just be doing up your breakfast things while the kettle boils. No, Sol, you sit with your friends," she ordered as Sol, rising, started gathering plates.

Sol said he wanted to help, and Mary said it wasn't necessary. Sol persisted, so Mary said he could slice the loaf. She pushed him down and Sol sat, looking puzzled. Luke said Sol had been right about one thing, Mary sure was something.

Seeing Sol's puzzled look deepen, Samantha followed his eyes to Mary. She had stopped at one of the seaward windows and seemed to be scanning the shoreline below. Then she spun on her heel, covered the distance to the sink in quick steps, literally dumped the dishes, hurriedly filled the kettle and put it on, grabbed some clean cups, and returned to the window for another look. Turning away, she found their eyes on her and, raising her chin, chirped, " 'Tis a lovely day," and trotted on to the table to plunk down the cups. "Cut nice

71

thick slices, now," she told Sol, shoving a knife into his hand. She returned to the sink.

Sol sat for a moment, considering the busy girl across the room, and then visibly shook off his contemplation and began cutting the still warm loaf of brown soda bread. "Mary's going to stay on and organize the reopening of O'Sullivan House," he said, as though he felt the need to straighten Mary's halo.

Luke cast a baleful eye at Mary. "Should be right up her alley."

Sol seemed to be examining the implication of Luke's remark, and Samantha, sensitive to the consequences of any ruffled feathers, hastily said, "Yes, indeed, she seems very efficient."

Sol's face cleared and he sent a fond glance across the room to the busy girl rattling teacups at the sideboard. "She is that. Do you know, she's lined up the villagers and assigned them all jobs to put the place in shape. Even the kids."

"My," Samantha said, feeling some comment was expected.

Sol sat up, as if struck with an idea. "We're going over there later this morning. There's to be a party Saturday night. Celebrating the start of the work. Would you two be coming along to help us figure out how to set it up?"

"I hope I'll be gone by then," Luke said.

"Me too," Samantha said. Hope was all she had left, it seemed.

The clattering tea tray heralded Mary's approach. She set down the tray and started pouring from the steaming teapot. "Here you are, then," she said, handing around cups. "There's nothing like a cup of good strong tea."

"You say that a lot, don't you?" Luke said.

For a split second Mary wavered, then continued, brighter than ever, " 'Tis true, you know. Strong tea and fresh-baked bread." She started lathering the thick slices of warm brown bread with creamy butter and chunky jam. "Do be having some," she invited Samantha as the slices piled up on the plate.

Samantha automatically started to refuse, then in a surge of self-pity thought, why not? She helped herself.

"I'm thinking that's enough bread, Mary," Sol said, eyeing the growing mound.

With a start Mary took in the heaped plate. "Oh. Yes. So 'tis." She scooped up the creamer. "So I'll just be filling the milk jug."

"Mary, the jug is full," Sol said.

"Then I'll just get it out of the way." She started to move off, but Sol grabbed her, looking at her with amazement.

"Mary, there is no lack of room on the table. Sit down."

"Here, take my place," Luke said, and moved to get up.

Mary shoved him down. "No, no. You've not had your tea. And here." She shoved the plate of bread at him.

"No, thank you, Mary." There was an edge to his voice.

"But—" Mary began.

"Oh, go ahead, have some," Samantha said, her mouth full. "It's delicious."

"Goddamn it!" Luke's chair scraped the floor. "I don't want to sit around here eating all morning. I want to get the hell on my way. Mary," he said, on his feet, "how soon before those bridges will be passable?"

"In a day or so," she began, reaching for his arm, but he sidestepped her.

"A day or so! Jesus Christ!"

Mary swiftly crossed herself. "In a day or so we'll be able to tell, I'm saying."

"What good would it do you anyway?" Samantha asked. "Your car is missing some tires, remember? And there's none to be had around here."

"One step at a time. When those bridges clear, I'll get some kind of transportation, you can bet." He began pacing around the kitchen.

Mary took off after him. "Perhaps they'll clear sooner. In the meantime—"

Sol, with a curious expression, sprang to his feet and grabbed her arm. "Mary," he said firmly, "let's go straighten the other rooms—"

"Not now, Sol." She shook off his arm and spun around to Luke. "Mr. Carter, won't you—" The words died on her lips. Luke had stopped before the same seaward window that she'd looked out of. She stood motionless, watching him.

Sol watched her watching Luke.

Samantha stopped chewing and looked up at the sudden silence. She looked from Sol to Mary to Luke.

Luke angrily drummed his fingers on the sill. All at once he stopped and his gaze seemed to focus on something down on the shore. After a moment's staring he said, "What the hell?" and pushed the window open and leaned out. "Sol," he called, his voice floating back into the room. "Sol, come here, will you?" Sol went over, and Luke pulled back into the room. "Take a look. I'll be goddamned if I don't see a body down there on the shore."

CHAPTER VIII

Samantha stopped licking jam off her thumb. "What did you say?"

Luke took a step away from the window, his expression one of astonishment. "There's a body washed onto the shore."

"Ho, boy," Sol said softly, his eyes going to Mary.

" 'Tis—'tis seaweed, most likely," she said, one hand at her throat.

Samantha eyed Luke skeptically. If the main topic of conversation over a period of twelve hours or so is mostly murder and dragnets, she supposed it was only natural to imagine bodies littering the landscape. She nodded at Mary. "Seaweed," she agreed, and resumed chewing, at the same time easing her waistband, which seemed to be tight all of a sudden.

Luke ducked out the window again and then pulled back in. "Seaweed, hell. Go ahead, Sol, look. That's a body, isn't it?"

Sol took a long look out the window and then turned away slowly.

Mary straightened. "Seaweed?" Her eyes dared contradiction.

"It's—it's—" Sol made a helpless gesture.

Samantha stopped chewing. "Don't tell me it's a body," she said on a rising note.

"See for yourself," Luke invited.

She shrank back. "No, thanks," she said, feeling the consternation that goes with a sudden plethora of bodies popping into one's life.

But Mary went to the window. She gave a brief glance, then turned away. "I'm thinking someone's had a drop too much and is only sleeping it off. It's best that we leave the poor fellow to his shame."

"That's a hell of a way to sleep off a drunk. Face-down, draped over a boulder. Looks to me as though the guy's dead or half dead. Come on, Sol, let's go see—"

"Just a minute." Mary's voice cracked like a whip, stopping the two men midstride. "It's the police who should be doing the investigating. We'd best get Father."

Samantha sat up. "Police?"

"And in the meantime the guy could be breathing his last." Luke got under way again. "Tell you what, you get your father, and we'll go on down to the beach. Come on, Sol."

"Police?" Samantha repeated in a wavering roupy voice.

Once more both men halted. "Christ," Luke said softly.

Sol bit his lip.

Mary crossed herself.

"Well . . ." Luke said irresolutely, "well . . . hell, maybe it is a drunk. We'll check him out, Mary. And it may be you won't have to bother your father. Come on, Sol."

"I'm going with you," Mary said, her look labeling Luke a troublemaker.

Left alone, Samantha sat for a moment, plunged in restless gloom. One minute life had been offering her ambrosia and honey and the next, moldy bread. Where would it all end? She unbuttoned her waistband, took an easier breath, and got to her feet, sending up a silent prayer that the fellow on the beach was alive—for his sake as well as her own. Another confrontation with Mr. Donegal was the last thing she wanted.

She went to the window, and her heart sank. The

form draped over the boulder looked very dead to her. She leaned weakly against the windowsill. The mournful squawk of the sea gulls circling the gray skies above the flat, leaden sea echoed her sense of despair. She took a deep breath. The air was damp and misty, smelling of moist earth.

Down below Luke, Sol, and Mary slipped and slid down the soggy, scree-covered slope. In a moment they crossed the rocky, boulder-strewn strip of shore to the lifeless form.

Before they reached it, however, Samantha saw Mary catch Luke's arm, and even from this distance Samantha could sense the intensity of her manner as she spoke to him. Or rather argued with him. For Luke was flinging his free arm around in what had become a familiar sign that things were not going as he wished. Sol simply stood off and seemed to be watching Mary. In the end Luke made a gesture of defeat and Mary released his arm.

Samantha expected the first thing to be done would be to check for vital signs like breathing or a pulse. Or the lack of them. Instead both Luke and Sol just squatted beside the body and studied it without even touching it. Then they got up, stood off, and studied it some more.

All of this Samantha thought strange behavior. But even more strange was that Mary seemed to show no interest in the victim at all.

While Luke and Sol were at least focusing their attention on the body, Mary was searching several hundred yards off to the right where a tree-covered point projected out into the water. From her vantage point Samantha could see a rowboat with five men huddled in it, lying just off the point, their oars idle.

Fishermen, she thought, and went back to watching Luke and Sol, now circling the form on the boulder.

Then Luke again got down on his haunches, and as he started to peer closer Samantha saw Mary turn abruptly and once more speak earnestly to both men. Then Luke slowly got to his feet, and after a few more words were exchanged, they all headed back up the slope.

Samantha went to meet them as, damp and muddy, they came around the corner of the cottage. "Is he—"

"Hard to tell," Luke said, not slowing his steps.

Samantha turned back to Sol and Mary, who were following more slowly. "What does he mean 'hard to tell'?"

"Well," Sol said, "he's lying facedown. But there's blood dried on the rock."

"Why didn't you check his pulse?"

"Mary didn't think we should touch anything."

Mary said nothing. She seemed deep in thought.

"Come on, let's go," Luke said impatiently over his shoulder, veering onto the path away from the cottage.

Samantha's stomach lurched. "You're going to get Mr. Donegal?"

Luke broke his purposeful stride. "Mary says we must."

Sol gave Samantha a meaningful look. "We'll probably go right down to the shore."

The word "probably" weighed heavily on Samantha's spirit. She took a ragged breath.

Sol took a closer look at her. "You all right?"

All right? She tried to smile.

Mary suddenly came to life. "Here, Sol, you take the car keys. I'll just stay with Mrs. Carter. She looks done in."

"Oh, no," Samantha protested, feeling any Donegal was a Donegal too many. "I mean . . . it's not necessary—"

"I'll not have it any other way," Mary said. "Come

78

along now. You're going to lie down, and I'll straighten up the kitchen."

And that was that. Samantha stood in the light drizzle, watching the two men drive off. Luke had certainly changed his tune about involvement. Mary tugged at her elbow. Samantha smiled weakly and followed her into the cottage and found herself ushered into the bedroom.

"Now you be slipping off your things and I'll be getting your dressing gown. It's in your case, is it?"

"Yes . . . no . . . that is, I'll just keep my clothes on. I'll only stretch out on top of the bed." All Mary would need was one look at her bra, Samantha realized. And then wouldn't the questions flow!

"Nonsense. That lovely suit'll get all wrinkled."

"It'll hang out. It's—it's warmer than my dressing gown and I feel a bit chilled."

"Oh, well, that's no problem. You can wear mine. It's—" Mary stopped. Her lips twitched. She shrugged. "Two years in London will prune a lot of ideas," she said without a trace of Irish lilt. She took a robe from the cupboard and held it out. It was not the sort one threw on to get the morning paper, and Samantha looked at Mary in a new light. However, now she was doing business at the same old stand once more. "Now get out of your things and I'll just be leaving you to your rest. It's no wonder you're that upset. Such a poor welcome from Ireland. The thieving tinkers and the—" She stopped and frowned. "Mrs. Carter, why are you and Mr. Carter traveling in two cars?"

It was a good question. All she needed now was a good answer. And she squandered a second in longing for the good old days when her greatest problem was whether to wear pearls and the black silk or the blue print with turquoise. One thing she was sure of. If she

79

ever got out of this mess, she'd never put a diamond in her jewel box. She never wanted to see one again. But in the meantime how to answer Mary? Why not a touch of the truth? The tart inner voice of Mary Samantha Malooly asked. "Uh . . . Luke had an appointment in one direction today, and I had one in the other."

"Oh?" Mary said with interest.

And for a moment Samantha thought, *Oh, God, she's going to pin me down.* But abruptly Mary's expression cleared and she turned on her heel and briskly made for the door. "Now, I'll just be in the kitchen if you're wanting—" She broke off and wheeled around. "You'll call if you're wanting anything, won't you? Don't get up and—" She took a breath. "I'm thinking it's best if you rest quietly. I'll look in on you from time to—"

"No, no. I'm sure I won't be wanting anything." Just peace and quiet, Samantha told herself. Just peace and quiet, please, for only half an hour or so.

Sol's expression had been thoughtful as he started up the car, and when he and Luke pulled away from the cottage, he sighed and said, "That's a tinker down there on the beach, Luke. Tinkers aren't very popular around these parts. Or in any settled community in Ireland for that matter. And a dead one means a heap of trouble."

"We're not sure he's dead though, are we? Mary saw to that."

Sol made no answer, and they drove in silence along the hedge-lined road until they came to an overgrown drive leading off to a big, square two-story Georgian house sitting on a rise, its many windows tightly boarded up. "O'Sullivan House," Sol said with a wave of the hand.

Luke roused himself and grunted.

A short distance on the road wound off to the right,

and midway along Sol pulled up before a smaller version of his own low whitewashed stone cottage. There was peat stacked handy to the door, lace curtains at the windows, and flowers along the path—rain-beaten but bravely giving color to the gray morning.

Mary's sister, Dierdre, was a slightly older edition of Mary. She greeted Sol, was pleased to meet Luke, and, after solemnly observing the Irish ritual of passing judgment on the weather, bade them enter. She offered each a cup of tea and a chair at the kitchen table, where her husband and father were finishing their breakfasts.

Hugh O'Callaghan, raw-boned and red-cheeked, pumped Luke's hand, and Mr. Donegal gave both callers a disgruntled eye that warned them that the memory of his interrupted sleep still rankled.

Luke refused both the tea and the chair, expecting that the news of a body in their midst would cause jumping to the feet and pushing to get out the door. He was mistaken. The only reaction was a quick swipe at the Sign of the Cross and a swift exchange of glances. A tiny whimper from an adjoining room sparked more of a flurry, Dierdre almost overturning her chair in her hurry to investigate. The Irishmen looked concerned until convinced the O'Callaghan heir's problem was in the natural order of things.

Once reassured, Mr. Donegal cleared his throat, leaned back in his chair, and took out a well-used pipe. "Tinker, you say?" He looked at Sol from beneath shaggy white brows.

"One by the name of Reilly, I'm thinking," Sol said.

Mr. Donegal carefully pressed tobacco into the curved-stem pipe. "Ah, yes. Them who broke down Sean Ward's fences Monday last."

"Dug his potatoes. Left the pit open, they did," Hugh said solemnly. "Ruined the lot. And the cattle scattered."

"Mr. Donegal, I don't think this is the time for chit-chat." Luke's tone was crisp. "There's a man dead or dying down on the shore, and it would seem to me, sir, that you'd better get over there and do whatever authorities do so the fellow can be moved."

Mr. Donegal didn't budge. He continued to pull on his pipe for a minute or so, then with a deceptively bland expression he said to Hugh. "This August last, it was, after the Puck Fair at Killorglin, they found the tinker Coffey dead by the roadside, did they not? Murdered, it was said, by one of the tribe of Reilly?"

"Aye. Got away he did. And still wanted by the gardai."

Mr. Donegal nodded. "I'm remembering. Bad business it was."

Hugh nodded. "Aye. Feuding. Fighting breaking out."

Mr. Donegal nodded. "And then the funeral."

Hugh nodded. "Camped on private property, they did. Set their animals grazing over the planted land. Opened up turf clumps and left them rifled and spoiling. Begging, stealing, and drinking. And all that fighting."

Mr. Donegal gave Luke a hard blue eye. "There are eighty-three people in Riverford, Mr. Carter. And no police force nearer than my two men a village away. We'd be no match for the large gathering of tinkers waiting out the storm in the back hills should they be stirred up over another killing."

Luke thought about that. Then he shook his head. "You can't just leave a man dying or dead on a beach."

A look passed between Hugh and Mr. Donegal. Hugh's eyes went to his watch.

" 'Tis a bad business," Mr. Donegal said, puffing away at his pipe as though he hadn't heard Luke.

"Aye," said Dierdre from the bedroom doorway. She

entered the room and joined her husband and father in thoughtful silence.

Luke tolerated a moment of this and then said tersely, "Don't you think we ought to get going?"

"Hugh," Dierdre said with sudden urgency in her voice, "the—the chickens. You're forgetting the storm blew down some of their shelter? It must be mended before the rain that's coming."

Hugh looked blank. "Chickens?"

Mr. Donegal looked pleased. "Ah, the chickens! Well, now, I'm thinking Sol here and Mr. Carter can be doing the quick mending while Hugh and I are getting Sean Ward. The Reilly men being that big, we'll be needing Sean Ward's van for moving the—"

"Now just a minute," Luke began in the firm voice of one not about to repair a hen house.

Dierdre cut him off. "It's that small a patch to be mended. It's better that Mr. Carter mind the baby while I gather the chickens that've scattered," she said all in a breath. "He'll be little trouble for he's sound asleep, the darling. And I'll not be gone long for I know for sure where the chickens will be."

Before Luke could open his mouth, Mr. Donegal took the car keys from Sol, summoned Hugh with a glance, and assured all from the doorway, "We'll be back in a jiffy."

CHAPTER IX

In the hills up behind Riverford the tinker Coffey sat half hidden in the grassy bank on the near side of High River. A big man with coarse, brutal features, his lips moved silently, laboring over the typewritten words on a single sheet of paper. Laboring or not, the fact that he was reading set him apart from his fellow tinkers. Few of them had even the little schooling Coffey had had thrust upon him.

It was not the first time during these early morning hours that Coffey had studied the document, but this time he completed it with the air of one satisfied at last that he fully understood its import. He carefully folded the paper in a lengthwise strip, reached for the grimy cloth cap lying on the grass beside him, and slid the strip into its loosened sweatband. Then he fitted the cap to his head, stretched out his legs, leaned back on his elbows, and considered the prospects that lay before him. He gave no thought—not even a dispassionate one —to the morning's happenings that had presented him with these prospects.

No matter to him the brief struggle on the river's bank, the random plunge of the knife into flesh, and the splash of a body into the swiftly coursing river. When he had come upon Reilly frowning over the typewritten paper, it had been merely a reflexive action to even things up with one of the clan who had killed his kinsman. Had he known what the harvest would be, he would have put a great deal more verve into the deed.

Fifty thousand dollars worth of diamonds! The words circled Coffey's brain. Fifty thousand dollars!

Coffey knew of no one in the whole of Ireland who had fifty dollars, let alone fifty thousand dollars. What that was in pounds he had no idea except that it would be more money than he dreamed anyone could have. He licked his lips and threw a glance over his shoulder to where a rickety two-wheeled cart lay partly concealed by a thicket. Six automobile tires were piled into the cart—four were from a small car, but the other two had been removed from a big car. Coffey was certain that only the very rich could afford a car like that. Someone rich enough to afford fifty thousand dollars worth of diamonds? He smiled to himself. The possibility was well worth looking into.

A horse neighed and Coffey wiped the smile from his lips. The sound came from the far bank at the shallow stretch a short distance farther up the river. Coffey quickly slid over on his stomach, the long thin blade of his pocketknife already out and at the ready. He guardedly raised his head and looked in the direction of the shallow stretch. He relaxed. The scrawny horse carried nothing but a small ragged girl—one of the horde of tinkers' children from the encampment farther back in the hills, on her way to a stint of begging in the village, he was thinking.

He pocketed his knife, rolled back on his elbows, and resumed his interrupted thoughts, his brow working with the effort of planning.

It was a busy morning, particularly for the five men whom Samantha had spotted earlier that morning laying to off the point. They were sprightly little old men with sharp, wizened faces—Hugh's uncles, the O'Callaghan Brothers everyone called them. At this moment their brows knitted with unwavering purpose and glistened with sweat, not at all surprising considering the burden four of them toted. The fifth uncle, who had a few more years on him than the others, scurried alongside and roundabout, cautioning and encouraging his brothers as they staggered up from the water's edge, bearing the dead weight of the tinker Reilly. They were veering and luffing toward a tangle of hedges growing unchecked just inside the low stone wall separating the lower grounds of O'Sullivan House from the beach.

"Mind you now the arm that is slippin'," the eldest warned. "Ah, there's dragging of the seat! Careful, careful, 'tis but a few steps we've got now."

His four brothers, with one mind, stopped and gauged the short distance remaining. Then, groaning and grunting, they resumed their heavy-burdened way, eventually pushing through the shrubbery and stopping just inside the untended lower gardens. With a minimum of conversation and a lot of labored breathing, the tinker was lowered and shoved in among the roots and branches of the shrubbery.

The group, panting and wheezing, paused in a tight little knot to eye the spot a moment or two, adjusting a bit of hedge here and there. Then the eldest gave a final wheeze and an "Ah, well" that served as a signal, and all the O'Sullivan Brothers silently threaded their way back out through the broken place in the wall back down to the rowboat at the water's edge.

Once their boat had cleared the beach, they worked their way around the point and into view of Sol's cottage. They laid down their oars, put out fishing lines, filled and lit their curly-stemmed pipes, and settled back. Now and again one would clear his voice, mutter "Ah, well . . ." and sigh and spit into the sea. The others would nod soberly and look back beyond the point.

Luke's brows had been working too; not with thought as Coffey's had, nor from effort as had the

O'Callaghan Brothers'. His worked with the anger born of frustration. Only fear of waking the sleeping infant kept him from pounding walls and kicking furniture. He had to content himself with mouthing curses and shaking his fist when he caught glimpses of Sol and Dierdre across the rain-soaked vegetable patches and berry bushes. Having taken Mr. Donegal's "We'll be back in a jiffy" at face value, he was discovering that an Irishman's "jiffy" tends to run to three quarters of an hour or so. Hugh and Mr. Donegal had been gone that long and Dierdre had apparently been getting all the mileage she could out of her captive handyman and baby-sitter.

When she finally followed Sol back to the cottage, it was with reluctant feet and the absent air of one wondering what else could be done.

With visible effort Luke kept his voice down as he lit into Sol. "Just what the hell is going on around here? Do you realize they've been gone over half an hour?" He turned on his heel. "Come on. I'm not waiting around here any longer."

Dierdre rushed to stop them. "Now, now, I'm that sure they'll be along any minute now. It's the van, I'm thinking, that's giving the trouble. Standing out in the storm, it was—"

"Then it's probably without tires," Luke said in the tone of one who should know. He tried to escape Dierdre's hand.

Dierdre held on. "There's Sean Ward's dog that'd be keeping the tinkers off. Come, sit down. I'll fix a nice fresh pot of tea."

"Oh, my God," Luke groaned softly. Then, firmly removing her hand, he said, "No tea, thank you, Dierdre. Tell your father and Hugh we've gone ahead."

"But—but . . . the road . . . it's that thick with mud. You'll ruin—" She took in what a morning's excursion down the muddy slope to the beach and a session around the hen house had wrought and switched midsentence. "But it's sure to start raining. You'll catch your death—" She found herself talking to a closing door.

Samantha had spent the intervening time revising a lot of old concepts. She had long concluded that in any group of idiots she'd come out well ahead of the pack. She was gazing morosely at the ceiling when she heard the front door bang and recognized Luke's particular style of pawing and snorting. Oh God, now what? She tiptoed to the door, listening for Mr. Donegal's voice, while weaving dreams of slipping out the window and heading for the hills to spend the rest of her days living on roots and berries. But then, remembering that these hills were full of tinkers and hearing no voices other than Luke's growl and Sol's murmurs, she went to the kitchen to see what Luke was breathing fire about.

Instead she found him standing humped in silence looking out the window down at the shore.

She sidled up to Sol, who was eyeing Mary, who was uneasily eyeing Luke. "Something wrong?"

"He's gone," Luke said gloomily.

"Who's gone?"

"The tinker—the guy on the beach."

"So? Wasn't that the main idea?"

"But we didn't move him," Luke said without turning around.

She went to the window and had a look for herself. Yes, indeed, there was no tinker draped on the boulder. "Was he a tinker?"

"He was a tinker," Sol said. "Name of Reilly."

She glanced around at the others. Why the solemn faces? Personally she found the seascape vastly improved. Bodies on rocks, she felt, were more to be regretted than missed. "What'd he do?" she asked Mary. "Just get up and walk off?"

Mary's eyes slid past Samantha's ear. "I—I was that busy at the sink. . . ."

Luke turned. "He went back into the water. Only it doesn't make sense. Why the hell would he go back into the water?"

"Why do you think he did?"

"Sol and I went down to look around and found splotches of fresh blood between the water and the boulder he'd been on."

Samantha took another look out the window and saw the rowboat with the five men in it. "Those men in the boat must've seen him leave. They've been out there all morning. I saw them earlier."

Luke snorted. "We almost waved our arms off trying to get them to come in, and all they did was wave back."

"They're Hugh's uncles—the O'Callaghan Brothers," Mary said. "And they're not to be counted on to know what happened. They're very old, and I'm thinking they have not the eyesight to see this far." She blandly met Sol's startled look and moved away from the window. "Well 'tis out of our hands now. That's a very strong current, you know." She picked up the teapot. "So why don't we—" She met Luke's baleful eye and set the teapot down. "—have a bit of music?" she finished smoothly, reaching for the transistor.

Samantha threw Luke a frantic expression. What with the law hot on her trail and the radio dial set on a news station quivering to reveal her identity to the world, she felt it was chancy to feed the information to someone who'd grown up in an atmosphere of *écrasez l'infâme*.

Luke got the message. "No, Mary, don't turn on the

radio. Uh . . . Samantha's headache. It's still bother-
ing you, isn't it, Samantha?"

She obliged him by putting a hand to her forehead
and looking pained.

"I'll tell you what, Mary," Luke said. "Why don't
you . . . uh . . . make some tea?"

Mary regarded him with pardonable surprise.
"You're wanting tea?"

His sigh was that of a trapped man, and he nodded,
unable to give word to the lie.

For a moment Mary stood, taking in the two of them
with an assessing eye that diminished the effect of be-
ribboned curls and dimpled cheeks. This Mary seemed
more at home behind an uncluttered desk, issuing
policy-making decisions, than over a hot stove, stirring
jams and baking loaves. In the next instant her expression cleared and she took a firm grip of the teapot and
headed for the stove when the doorknocker sounded.
"Ah, that'll be Father," she said.

Samantha was off the mark in a flash. "I—I think
I'll lie down again," she said, brushing past Mary.
"My—my headache. . . ." The words floated back
into the room as she disappeared around the door.

For the second time within minutes, Mary studied
the situation. As the light of suspicion in her eyes grew
stronger, Luke frowned and Sol gave a nervous twitch.
Then Mary resolutely set the teapot down. "See to the
door, Sol. I'm going in to Mrs. Carter."

Luke took a quick step. "I don't think—"

"I don't imagine you do," she said and sailed out of
the room.

Luke dragged a hand over his unshaven jaw. "I got a
feeling—"

"—it's about to hit the fan," Sol finished, shudder-
ing.

The doorknocker banged again.

CHAPTER X

Sol admitted Hugh and Mr. Donegal. The pourparlers were deftly dealt with and the business at hand got down to, namely the missing body.

"Gone, you say?" Mr. Donegal's round rosy face was a study in surprise. "Now, what do you make of that? You're sure it was there in the first place, are you?"

"It was there, all right," Luke said stiffly. "And shall we get on down there and—"

"Whatever for?" Mr. Donegal wanted to know. "The man's gone, you say."

"You don't believe there was a body, is that it?" Luke's face was darkening by the minute.

"Did anyone else see it?" Mr. Donegal asked mildly.

Before Luke could take a swing at the neat evasion, Sol stepped in. "Mary saw it. She went down to the shore with us."

"Ah, yes, Mary." Mr. Donegal looked around. "And where might she be now? And Mrs. Carter?"

"They're in the bedroom," Luke said. He gave an uneasy glance in the direction of the passageway, as though expecting to see Mary striding out, leading a penitent Samantha ready to tell all. "My . . . uh . . . Samantha isn't feeling well and Mary's . . . seeing to her."

"Not feeling well, is she? And no wonder. Getting her out in the early morning weather. And in her condition."

"Condition?"

But Mr. Donegal had dismissed Luke and turned his attention to Hugh. "Come along, then. We'll be going down to see whatever is to be seen." He started towards the door, then turned. "Solomon, will you be telling Mary—" He frowned, finding Luke and Sol trailing Hugh. "Now there's not the need for you to come."

"Don't you want us to show you where we found the body?" Luke said. "And the way it was positioned?"

"I'm assuming there's but one boulder with blood on it. Unless you've found others since your return?" Mr. Donegal's look implied Luke was easily the sort to litter Irish beaches with imaginary bloodied boulders.

"There was only one boulder." A muscle in Luke's jaw tightened.

"And you did say the supposed body was, let's see, I'm thinking 'sprawled' was the way you put it?"

"Sprawled." Luke said crisply.

"Well, then, if there is a boulder to be found with blood on it—blood from a sprawled body, that is— we'll be making the note of it." Ticking off Luke and his busy jaw, Mr. Donegal fixed his bright blue eyes on Sol. "I'll be leaving the car for Mary with the word that Dierdre's said she can manage without her. Will you be telling her that? And that there's not the need for her to worry, we've the use of the van of Sean Ward for all the need we'll have of it. Will you not be forgetting to tell her just that?"

"Yes, sir . . . I mean no, sir . . . I mean I'll not be forgetting, sir." Sol said. "We'll be glad for the car, sir, else we'd be walking to O'Sullivan House—"

Hugh gave a start, and he and Mr. Donegal stopped dead. "O'Sullivan House?" Hugh said.

"And what might you be going there for?" Mr. Donegal wanted to know.

"We've things to see to. There's the gathering this weekend, you know. The celebrating of the beginning of the remodeling . . . ?"

"The gathering . . ." Hugh said hollowly. He and Mr. Donegal exchanged a look.

"Ah, yes, well come along, Hugh. We've a full morning ahead."

Hugh leaped after Mr. Donegal, slamming the door behind them.

"What put them in high gear?" Luke said sourly.

Sol shrugged. "Who knows?" He shifted his position and glanced down the hallway. "What do you think is going on in there?"

Luke pulled himself up and, sighing deeply, went to the bedroom door. He started to knock, then hesitated. He put his ear to the door, listened a moment, then backed off. In answer to Sol's inquiring eyebrows, he gave an uncertain shake of the head and went on into the kitchen. Sol followed.

"Hear anything?"

"Murmuring. And sniffling."

"Why didn't you go on in?"

"Because I don't know that I could keep from spouting off if Samantha's still protecting that guy. She'd probably do better on a woman-to-woman basis. Anyway women with the upper hand scare me. And your Mary has a firm little jaw." He plunged his hands into his pockets. "You know, you and I aren't going to come off smelling like roses. What's the penalty for aiding and abetting a fugitive in Ireland?"

"For me it'll probably be the rack," Sol said and wandered over to the window.

Luke stood jingling coins in his pocket a moment and then joined Sol.

A watery sun was bravely trying to break through the overcast sky; the seabirds were still circling over the slippery-looking sea, though now and then one would swoop down at the rowboat in which the five old men still drifted offshore. Mr. Donegal was making slow progress covering the last few feet of the slope. Upon reaching the pebbled flat, he brushed aside Hugh's helping hand and stood a moment, apparently catching his breath. Hugh went on to the water's edge and began waving at the five old men.

"That's a waste of time," Luke said. Then, perking up: "How the hell do you like that?" he demanded as the O'Callaghan Brothers picked up their oars and began rowing toward shore—that is, four rowed and one flapped.

"Don't forget, they're Hugh's uncles," Sol said, but he watched curiously.

Mr. Donegal joined Hugh at the water's edge, and they spoke, heads together, for a moment or so, and then Mr. Donegal threw a glance back up toward the cottage. He said something more to Hugh before trudging over to the large boulder where the tinker had lain. He walked once around it, pulled out a notebook and jotted in it, flung another glance up at the cottage, and marched back to the water's edge.

"Some investigation," Luke said.

"Knew exactly which boulder to check, though, didn't he," Sol said, continuing to watch with a thoughtful eye.

When the rowboat neared, Hugh waded out and pulled it onto shore. A short confab followed, and then Mr. Donegal climbed into the boat and Hugh pushed it back into the flat gray water. He stood watching the rowers sort themselves out and then, as soon as the boat began moving unsteadily toward the tree-covered jetty of land, he turned abruptly and scrambled back up the slope.

"That's a hell of a way to search for a body," Luke said when the boat was well underway. "They're taking a straight course to that finger of land."

Sol merely grunted and continued thoughtfully to watch the boat's progress.

The sound of the van's motor springing to life roused both of them. As it spurted off Luke shook his head.

"Ah, well . . . " he said, mimicking Mr. Donegal perfectly, "to hell with it. I've got problems of my own. And Samantha'll at least have time to calm down before facing Mr. Donegal—if that's to be the next step." He went to the doorway and stood, listening for a moment. Then, shrugging, he walked over to the fireplace and dropped into a chair.

He and Sol were sitting before the ashes of last night's fire, studying the toes of their shoes when the bedroom door opened. It had opened once or twice before and they had sat up, straight and alert, but the footsteps had gone only as far as the bathroom each time. This time, however, there was the murmur of approaching voices—Mary's firmly encouraging, Samantha's reluctant. The men were on their feet when Mary appeared in the doorway.

She raked Sol with an accusing eye. "All right now," she said in the crisp tone of a field general straightening out the troops, "I've the whole story." She pinned Luke's ears back with a look. "You men! One can always count on you to muddy the waters. Samantha's done nothing so why should she go taking the blame and ruining her life for the likes of you? Let's have no more talk of it," she said, stopping Luke's attempt to get a word in. "We'll keep her safely hidden here in Riverford until the real villain is caught." She said this as though it was something she could do with no questions asked. That being that, she turned to look in Samantha's direction. "Come along, there's none but the two of them here. Come show them what we've done."

In Luke's wide experience with women he had learned long ago that what you see is not always what you get. Over the years he had acquired a certain finesse in handling the moment of truth. So he really knew better than to gasp "My God" when Samantha dragged herself into view.

95

Samantha folded her arms and leaned against the doorjamb, bleakly accepting his reaction. She knew it wasn't so much, that she'd been stripped of her thirty-five-dollar eyelashes and that her face had been scrubbed bare of any makeup. It was more that her long blond hair had been chopped off by an amateur hand wielding dull scissors and that it approximated the color of mud.

"You—you look . . . different," Luke said, putting it in a nutshell.

"That's the whole idea," Mary said, pleased. "She'll not now be recognized by any who've heard the broadcast, I'm thinking."

"You're certainly right there," Luke said.

"Watercolors," Mary said, revealing the secret of her success. "I used Sol's watercolors on her hair."

Samantha drew a shaky breath.

Sol pulled himself together. "You look fine, just fine," he told Samantha stoutly, and his smile patted her shoulder.

She looked at him. "You're a nice person, Sol," she said.

With a belated sense of the occasion Luke said heartily, "You do look fine. Really. More . . . natural. Wholesome," he added, not knowing when to quit.

"Great," she said and moved away from the door.

They all stood around like people who have exhausted a topic and don't know what to say next.

Sol came up with an idea. "What do you say we give the new you a trial run? Go over to O'Sullivan House while the weather holds? You'll feel better for the fresh air and a change of—"

"No!" Mary said sharply. "I mean"—she put a smile on her face and the Irish back in her voice—"I've a better idea. We'll go to the Emporium and see if the telephones are back in service."

96

"I don't think we'd find it open," Sol said. "I think Hugh's busy with your father." He held her eye. "Wouldn't they be searching for the tinker now?"

She carefully looked away. "Yes, they would that, I'm sure. But I've Hugh's keys and I'm thinking"—she turned to Samantha, the lilt going full blast—"I'm thinking if you call Parknasilla and leave a message with the desk that you've met with problems and will not be arriving, it will be stopping any search your people might make."

"And pinpointing where she is for the desk clerk to tip off the police when Amsterdam comes up with her name, as they're expecting to," Luke said.

"Not so," Mary said. "The name Amsterdam will come up with is not Samantha Malloy but Mary Samantha Malooly, her real name that's given on her passport."

Luke looked at Samantha. "Malooly? Mary Malooly?"

Sol's grin was wide. "Never you say!"

Samantha's chin went up. "Yes. Mary Samantha Malooly. Samantha Malloy is my professional name. And my mother was a Ryan," she added for good measure.

"It figures," Luke said.

A glint came into her eye. "What do you mean by that?" Her tone was pure Malooly.

"It's just something about the oblique manner in which the Irish seem to approach their problems," he said with a shake of his head. Then he grew brisk. "Okay, I've got some important calls to make too, you know. Not that I really expect the phones'll be working. But let's get going anyway."

Samantha tugged at her bra, stalling. She had little enthusiasm for venturing into the outside world. When one's faith in the power of beauty borders on the mystical, it's difficult to face the public at large, looking like something the mice have been at. "I—I don't think I should wander around with Warren's diamonds," she said. She wriggled inside her bra. "I think the elastic's losing its stretch. Maybe I'd better stay here and you make the call for me, Mary."

But it seemed Mary's voice would be recognized by the Parknasilla personnel, and the general opinion was that it would be best that no edge be given anyone tracking down Samantha.

"I'll grab if any slipping starts," Luke offered.

Samantha treated him to a cold eye.

"You could stash your loot someplace around the house," Sol suggested.

She turned the idea briefly in her mind. No, the way things were going, it would be just her luck to have Riverford break out in a crime wave with Sol's cottage burgled first. Warren had said she must keep the stones with her, and she'd do so until the police took them away from her. "No, I'll keep them with me, as I promised, even though I'll probably be recognized by the first person we come across and have to turn them over to the authorities."

"I don't think there's much danger that you'll be recognized," Luke said.

"There'll be no one about the village yet," Sol put in hastily. "After a storm there's lots to be done at home first thing. And we'll go right on to O'Sullivan House, so it's not likely you'll come across anyone else all day."

A lot he knew.

CHAPTER XI

With sagging shoulders and lifeless step, Samantha followed the others out the door and down the soggy path. Though she sported an oilskin hat of Sol's as protection against the weather's adverse effect on her watercolored hair, it bobbed loosely and the damp air settled about her naked ears and face. If at this precise moment she'd come upon Warren being set upon by thugs, before she'd have gone to his aid she'd have seen that he'd been dealt a good solid blow or two first. Lost in the thought, she stumbled into Sol, who, with Luke and Mary, had stopped for a moment's silence at the little tireless car.

"Why just the tires?" Luke said as they sorted themselves into the Donegal car. "Why not swipe the whole car?"

"It's the small stuff the tinkers prefer," Sol said as Mary, behind the wheel, took her time about getting the car keys out and the seat adjusted to her liking. "They mostly steal anything that's lying around loose and unguarded if it's not very distinctive and has scrap value. And of course foodstuffs. Chickens, eggs, milk, like that," he added abstractedly, his eye on Mary as she selected the proper key through an elaborate process of elimination.

"Take it from me, they're branching out into things that are attached. Like tires," Luke said, looking big and out of place in the backseat. He squirmed restlessly. "Come on, Mary, let's get going."

"Ah, here's the key. The last one, would you be knowing?" She fitted the key into the ignition and began fussing with the rearview mirror.

"You'll be twisting it off its mooring," Sol said after a moment.

She cursed him with a look but started the car, and they headed up the lane.

It was the same lane, Samantha observed, that she had so blithely driven down the night before. Only the night before? God, it seemed a lifetime ago. She pushed the oilskin hat out of her eyes and huddled deeper into her corner. Once more the hat slid forward. Sighing, she shoved it back again. Just one more cross. She stared gloomily out the window, finding no joy in the daylight show of white hawthorn jumbled with fiery-red fuchsias growing wild through the high, thick hedges bordering both sides.

At the top of the lane they halted at the ditched Jaguar, bereft of its tires. Everyone gave it a moment of silence—except for Luke, who used up the time in colorful comments on the antecedents of tinkers in general. "Why the hell don't the people around here go up into the hills and clear the bastards out or throw them in jail?"

"They'll be leaving when the storm's passed," Mary said. "Besides, we've neither the men to do the job nor a jail to put them in."

Samantha perked up. "No jail?"

"We get little need for it," Sol said.

"Your police force being what it is, no doubt," Luke said.

Samantha sat a little more comfortably and took more interest in her surroundings as Mary put the car in gear, slowly turned off the lane, and proceeded onto the road. Anyplace without a jail was an all-right place with her. In a moment they were in the village. And almost through it.

❖　❖　❖

One glance told Samantha why Riverford hadn't appeared on the map. She wondered how it had even rated a directional sign.

The rutted road ran between six or seven cottages and shops on the one side and a mix of hedgerows and stone fences overgrown with sod and grass, all ablaze with fuchsias, on the other. Then it wound along for a bit till it came to a little old church beside an equally old graveyard, where no two headstones leaned at the same angle. Then it rose up and over a very old bridge and trailed from sight.

It was an old village and a poor village. But it wore its aged poverty with a comfortable air. Each cottage had been faithfully rethatched, mended, and painted over the years, and each had a quaint garden. The shops too had been faithfully patched, shored, and painted; their windows stoutly framed; and the merchant's name boldly lettered on the fascia boards: MCCARTHY BUTCHER, CASEY GROCER, WARD FRUITERERS. On the building that Mary pulled up to hung a sign saying O'CALLAGHAN'S EMPORIUM.

Samantha could now see that Sol knew what he was talking about when he said the Irish were reluctant to start the day. Not only was there no sign of life in any of the small shops, but there were no villagers abroad to notice it.

"I'll be damned," Luke said, getting out and looking up and down the deserted street. "Not a soul in sight and the morning practically gone."

"The Irish hate getting up on the best of mornings," Sol said. "And with the devil's own storm these past two days, only the desperate or the daft would venture out not knowing 'twas done with."

No sooner had the words left his lips than the *clip clop* of a horse's hooves broke the morning stillness. Sol and Luke turned in the direction of the sound, and Samantha and Mary got out of the car just in time to see an unkempt, ferret-faced little girl astride a bony nag emerge from the alleyway alongside O'Callaghan's.

"It's a tinker," Mary said, pressing her lips together.

"Tinker?" Samantha clutched her diamonds and crowded behind Luke.

At sight of the four adults, the child urged her horse toward them and, thrusting down a dirty hand, whined, "Could you be sparing a copper, your Honors, in the name of the Holy Saints? And I will be remembering you in my prayers."

Luke fished in his pockets. "There'd be more than a copper in it for you if you'd find some missing tires for me," he said, pulling out a handful of coins.

Samantha gave him marks for fast thinking.

"Tires?" The sharp little eyes narrowed. "Aye, you be giving me a bob and I'll be fetching them for you."

"Oh, no," Luke said. "You fetch the tires and then the bob."

The dirty little face tightened craftily. "Please, sir, if you'll be telling me how many you're wanting—"

"Six," Samantha said quickly.

Luke considered the child. "Get some new tires up at the fork this morning?"

The child drew herself up. "The fork? I'll not be of the likes of them that camp amongst the Coffeys," she spat.

Mary quickly stepped up. "And what'll be the name of your clan?"

"We be the clan of Reilly," she said, her attention back on the coins in Luke's hand.

"And where are the Reillys camping?" Sol said softly.

The child's eyes darted among the coins. "We be just down the road."

Samantha pounced on the information. She moved from behind Luke. "How did you get across the river?"

"At the low place." Her face puckered with sudden remembrance, and she looked around her. "I'm after finding my da. Would you be seeing him?"

Samantha's heart quickened. Low place! If there was a low place into Riverford, there was a low place out of Riverford.

Luke was just a hair's breadth ahead of her. "Just where is this low—" He stopped short. "Your da?" he said. "Would that be your father?" When she said it would be, he looked at Sol. "Reilly?"

Sol barely nodded.

Samantha, weighing the chances of buying the child's horse and striking out for the low place and Parknasilla, became aware of a sudden silence. She looked from one to the other of her companions and found them regarding the child with varying dregrees of cautious interest.

"Your father's gone off?" Luke asked carefully.

"There's none has seen him since early daylight and him rousing Brother to read a paper he found." She grew proud. "It was a good priest taught Brother reading in pris—" She decided against this bit of family background. "Brother can read. Big words there was too. Brother said 'twas all about diamonds."

The reaction was unanimous.

There was a moment's awed silence among the adults, during which everyone slid glances at everyone else. Then Samantha said in a tight little voice, "Diamonds?"

Luke stepped in, jingling the coins in his fist. "Diamonds is a big word. Were there other big words?"

"Aye," she said, her eyes glittering greedily, watching his hand. "More big words, and I was hearing him read big numbers."

103

"And does your brother have this paper?" Luke asked carefully.

"He does not. Please sir," she wheedled, "you'll be giving me the coppers now and I'll be leaving wishing God's blessings on you."

Luke slowly paid out the coins. "Now about—"

But with the clink of the last coin he lost the ear of the recipient and everything connected with it. The scruffy little child had kicked her heels into the horse and the next moment was thudding back up the alley.

"Hey," Luke shouted after her, "where—"

"You're wasting your breath. You'll not be seeing any more of that one," Mary said.

"Hell, I didn't even get my God's blessing."

They all stared where the child had been for a moment, then Luke said, "Where's this low place?"

"That I don't know. Though there is one, we've heard," Mary said.

Luke turned to Sol in exasperation. "Well, who would know?"

"I don't think anyone's looked for it."

"Why should they?" Mary wanted to know.

Luke gave her a look of utter disgust. "For one thing, at a time like this it'd be damned convenient to be able to get out of town if you had to."

"I suppose," Mary allowed. "Only nobody's ever had to."

"Oh, my God," Luke groaned, "if you people don't take—"

Samantha jabbed him. "Will you tell me just why we are wasting time with a nowhere conversation when we could start looking for that tinker with my bill of sale!"

The others turned to her, as though she'd sprung up out of the ground. "That particular tinker is the bird we found on the rock this morning," Luke said.

"Oh, no!"

Sol nodded solemnly.

Samantha drew a breath and looked away. "Ah, well . . ."

There was a flicker of reappraisal in Luke's eyes as he considered her for a moment. Then they all trudged into O'Callaghan's Emporium.

It was the Irish version of the American general store of bygone days. Hand plows and farm implements, shelves of dry goods. There was a hardware section, a toy bin or two. A glass-enclosed showcase displayed gimcracks and souvenirs—apparently on the odd chance a tourist stumbled into the village. In the middle of the crowded area stood racks of shirts and dresses, counters of sturdy shoes and no-nonsense sweaters. And tucked into a corner next to a cubicle lettered POST OFFICE was the pay telephone.

"You first," Luke said and offered to place Samantha's call.

Putting through a coin-box call in Ireland is not a simple matter of shoving a coin in the proper slot and getting on with the dialing. It is a complex system of coin slots, beeps, "A" buttons, "B" buttons, and a lot of luck. But Luke had no chance to lick the complicated routine because no amount of coin depositing or button pushing brought life to the instrument.

"It's no use," he said at last, abandoning the jangling and clanging of coppers and helloing into the mouthpiece. "Deader than a doornail." He heaped a dozen or so words of displeasure on the mute instrument and turned away. "Well, let's go have a look at the bridges. Just for the hell of it, of course."

They straggled through the clutter of the Emporium. Luke cast an eye about. "Everything but tires, I see," he said gloomily.

Samantha's glance flickered over the rack of dresses—all eight or nine garments. She'd have to do something about a change of clothes before long. Warren's instructions that she send her own luggage along with that of her colleagues from New York to save time collecting it at Schiphol was added to the pile of bones she had to pick with him.

Naturally the water had not gone down. Barricades blocked the path of anyone foolhardy enough to try to cross either of the sagging and partially submerged wooden structures. Signs of ancient vintage crudely lettered UNDERWATER hung from the barricades of both bridges and led one to believe the condition was not a new one to the villagers.

At High River Bridge Luke shook his head in amazement. "Did anyone ever give a thought to replacing these prehistoric monstrosities?"

"It's been mentioned," Mary said. "Particularly after such a storm. But then the water goes down and so does the idea."

"And so will a villager one of these days. Has anyone ever thought of that?" Luke said.

Mary looked at the barely visible wooden structure. "H'mm. You're an expert, are you?"

"You may quote me."

"Build bridges, do you?"

"Among other things."

"H'mm," she said again, regarding him thoughtfully.

"So shall we get on to O'Sullivan House?" Sol said. Mary frowned.

"If you don't want to go, Mary," he said, "we can walk over. If you're worrying about Dierdre doing without you—"

"No, no." She led the way back to the car.

Samantha climbed into her corner and shoved back

the oilskin hat, pushing a straggle of hair off her forehead. Her fingers came away rancid-coffee colored. At least, she thought, she'd been spared the humiliation of any villagers seeing her. And Sol had said there'd be no one at O'Sullivan House to stare at her either.

But he was wrong.

While the four of them drove toward O'Sullivan House, Mr. Donegal, Hugh, and the O'Callaghan Brothers were already there. Mr. Donegal stood glaring while the others poked and prodded the shrubbery against the seawall.

"It's that you've forgotten where you laid him," he was saying to the five little old men. "Think, think."

The eldest of the O'Callaghan Brothers straightened, glinty eyed. "And I'm telling ye 'twas right here we left him. And he's up and gone."

CHAPTER XII

Mary drove onto the weed-choked gravel sweep of O'Sullivan House and carefully turned off the ignition. As they piled out of the car, she glanced around apprehensively. Sol glanced around critically, Luke, curiously, and Samantha, openmouthed.

O'Sullivan House loomed huge. A two-story Georgian affair, it was built of gray stone, now ivy-clad and moss-covered, with several chimneys protruding from its heavy slate roof and the whole riding high on wide stone terraces. Though its surrounding grounds had gone wild and its many windows and doors were boarded, it did not have the look of a place abandoned but simply of one biding its time.

Samantha was impressed. Mounting the flight of stone steps onto the terrace, she wished she were in charge of dishing out the plums of this world; she'd see to it that the proper type got manor houses and not sandal-footed youths who preferred to live in thatched cottages.

Mary took the lead, striking a high trot for the rear terrace, the others straggling in her wake. Luke looked over the balustrade at the tangle of tall grasses, shrubbery, and neglected flower beds. "When is this shindig you're planning?"

"This weekend," Sol said.

"Aren't you afraid you'll lose some of your guests in that jungle down there?"

"Oh, we'll get a work crew busy with scythes and whatever in the next day or so."

"Believe in waiting until the last minute, do you?"

" 'Tis the Irish way," Sol said, grinning.

"I could wind up with ulcers, working in this country," Luke said gloomily.

"On the other hand you might come off without a nerve in your body."

Luke dismissed that possibility with a look.

Mary wore a perplexed, uncertain air when they came up to her, but she quickly slipped on a smile for the troops. "Shall we start taking down the boards?" She made a little ushering gesture away from the edge of the terrace.

"Take down the boards? Why would we do that when it's the ground we've got to work on?" Sol asked.

" 'Tis the Irish way," Luke murmured and joined Samantha at the balustrade while Mary looked on nervously.

The grounds fanned out before them, screened either side by hedges and trees all the way down to the barely glimpsed seawall, the sweep of land just below the terrace sloping gently down to the long-neglected lower gardens, ending at the hedges growing inside the seawall; beyond, the sea wrinkled and creamed onto a strip of rocky shore. As Luke and Samantha admired the view a black-suited figure emerged onto the beach from the shelter of the lower hedges and headed off to the right.

"Hey, isn't that your father down there, Mary?" Luke said.

"It—it does look like him," she said. As she spoke another figure appeared and then one by one five more trooped out of the hedges and off down the beach.

"Hugh and the O'Callaghan Brothers," Sol announced.

"I wonder . . ." Luke said with quickened interest. "Do you suppose they found the tinker?" He got under way. "Let's go find out."

"They'd be gone before you could reach them," Mary said quickly.

But Luke was not to be denied. Any voice that could carry over the raucous din of heavy-duty earth-moving machinery found no difficulty catching the ear on a still Irish morning with only a quiet surf as competition.

The men on the beach stopped and looked all around.

"Hold it," Luke bellowed.

They finally located the source.

"Come on, Sol," Luke took the terrace steps two at a time.

Mary sprang to life and grabbed at Sol's arm. "Sol— She glanced at Samantha, and though she saw her attention was riveted on the men on the beach, Mary drew Sol a step or so farther away. "Sol," she said, hesitant and uncertain. "They've—they've done what they think best. . . ."

Sol's eyes flickered.

She swallowed. "We only meant to put off . . . that is . . . when the rivers go down—"

Sol nodded, half to himself. "I figured something like that." He patted her hand. "Don't worry, he said, and was off.

Luke reached the hedges as Sol covered the last few feet of the slope. "How do we get out?" he asked Sol.

"There's an opening." Sol, panting, moved on ahead, glancing sharply along the hedges as he followed broken branches and trampled ground. He found the gate and they pushed their way onto the beach.

The O'Callaghan Brothers were climbing into Sean Ward's van parked at the end of a muddy track that paralleled the outer side of the windbreak. Mr. Donegal watched Luke and Sol approach, Hugh at his elbow.

Never one to stand on ceremony, Luke got right down to business. "Did you find the tinker?"

"We did not," Mr. Donegal stated flatly with a look that dared the American to start something.

Luke shot a thumb at the O'Callaghan Brothers. "Did they say anything about spotting him when they were fishing earlier?"

"They did not."

"Did not see him or did not say?" Luke said, his question taking in Hugh as well.

Hugh looked away.

"They know nothing of the whereabouts of the tinker," Mr. Donegal said.

Luke gave him a long look, then shrugged. "I see. Well, that would seem to be that, wouldn't it."

"It would so," Mr. Donegal said in a voice as smooth as butter. "If that's all you were wanting to know, we'll be off." He gave Hugh the signal, and they resumed their way. As they neared the van, a grinding of gears heralded the approach of a car coming down the track. In a moment it came into view, and Mr. Donegal and Hugh hurried to meet it.

"Who's that?" Luke asked Sol.

"City fathers," Sol said, considering the three men in the car and the covert glances they were sending Sol and Luke as they listened to Mr. Donegal.

"If, as you say, only the desperate or daft venture out in this weather, what are they? Desperate or daft?" Luke asked.

"Like I also say, who can tell from the Irish?"

The discussion at the car was a short one, and Mr. Donegal and Hugh returned to the van. In a moment both cars had made the turn and headed back up the track.

"Yes, sir," Luke said, following Sol through the choked opening back into the lower gardens, "a lot of people seem to be stirring about early this morning, all right." Once inside the grounds he regarded the thick growth along the seawall. "I'm going to have a look around here."

"What for?"

"Just for the hell of it."

Sol met his eyes and threw in the towel. "Think they stashed him here, do you?"

"That's just what I'm thinking."

Sol sighed and looked off up at the terrace where the two women were watching, while Luke began searching the hedges. When Luke called out, "Look here, Sol," his shoulders drooped and he trudged over with bowed head.

Luke, down on his haunches, pointed to broken branches and trampled leaves. "Have a look."

Sol got down beside him. "Could have been kids," he said finally.

Luke peered deeper inside the hedge, then reached in and brought out a broken branch. Blood stained the leaves.

"And then again it could've been a bleeding tinker," Sol said resignedly.

He joined Luke, poking and prying farther through the hedges but found nothing more.

"Where could he have gone?" Luke asked as they made their way back up the slope.

"Who can tell? Tinkers know more about hiding places around a town than the villagers who've lived in them all their lives."

Mary took an uncertain step in their direction when they reached the terrace, and Sol drew her off to one side, while Luke went over to where Samantha stood, anchoring her oilskin hat with one hand and clutching her diamonds with the other. "Where's Mr. Donegal?" she asked nervously.

"He's gone."

She took off the hat and fanned herself with it.

"You make a rotten fugitive," he said. "And you'd better put your hat back on before your disguise runs."

She hastily crammed the hat back on.

He looked closer at her. "You don't make a bad-looking brunet."

"My roots'll be thrilled to know," she said bleakly and got a quick surprised smile out of him. "You have a nice smile," she said.

"Thank you. Care to go on from there?"

"No, that's about it, I guess."

"Drat."

By the time she looked away there had been a subtle shift in their relationship. She leaned against the balustrade. "What were you looking for down in the hedges?"

"A grave."

"A grave!"

"Or a body."

"I hate the way that word keeps popping up in our conversation," she said. "You mean the tinker, I sup—" She gasped. "Luke, my receipt! He's got—"

"Forget it. We didn't find him."

Her face fell. "Why did you think you would in the first place?" she asked after a moment's disappointed reflection.

"Just a hunch. And I was right. He'd been there."

"How do you know?"

"Blood on the leaves."

"Oh, why doesn't he stay put!"

"Because the police are after him. You know how it is."

She let that go by. "Am I supposed to stand here and feed you lines or are you going to tell me what's going on?"

He looked over at Mary and Sol, deep in conversation. "Well, the way I figure it, this tinker Reilly is supposed to have murdered some tinker from another clan, and somebody from that clan tried to even things up this morning. And the whole of Riverford's got a hair up—uh—everybody's spooked because they're not equipped to handle feuding and fighting just now. So my guess is they planned to stash the body away quietly. Only . . ." He spread his hands.

"Only there is no body. But there are a couple of murder suspects wandering around the place now, aren't there?"

"Actually," he said with a knowing look, "there are three, if you're counting—"

"Don't say it, just don't say it." She shoved the floppy hat back, turned around, and leaned back against the balustrade. "I don't think I can handle any more worries," she said wearily.

"You could eliminate a big one with only a word to Mr. Donegal, you know."

She couldn't see how that would accomplish anything more than get herself photographed above a number. She shook her head.

"For Christ's sake, Samantha, why don't you stop thinking about that Warren creep and start thinking—"

"Oh, to hell with Warren. It's not him," she said without thinking. And then she stopped to think. To hell with Warren?

"Well, now, let's build on that thought," Luke said approvingly.

To hell with Warren? She moved slowly away from the balustrade, trying to dredge up a sense of guilt, disloyalty, or something. Nothing. She stopped before a boarded window, and Luke loomed up beside her. She put her face up to a wide crack in the board. She needed to do some thinking, all right, but not with Luke watching her.

114

"So if that's the way you feel about him, why not have that little chat with Mr. Donegal?" Luke said.

"I'll—I'll think about it," she said, peering through the crack into the gloom inside. "This window's broken," she said with the hope of changing the subject. "Sol'd better get it fixed before the—"

"Never mind the window. What's there to think about, tell me. Just go to Mr. Donegal and—"

"And tell him what? That the police in Amsterdam want to question me about a murdered diamond broker and two hundred and fifty thousand dollars worth of missing diamonds? When I can't prove I didn't murder the man? And do you think he'd believe I don't know anything about two hundred and fifty thousand dollars worth of diamonds when I have fifty thousand dollars worth tucked in my bra that I can't prove I bought because I've lost the bill of sale? He'd throw me in jail so fast—"

A sharp splintering sound, like a footstep on broken glass, came from the other side of the boarded window.

There was an electrified second of silence. Then Samantha clutched Luke's arm. "Wha—what was that?"

"Mice, I guess," he said a shade too glibly, then, shooting her a warning look, drew her out of range of the boarded window.

She felt the tension in his fingers as he pulled her along to the far side of the terrace. "Luke, was it the tinker?" she whispered.

"Five'll get you ten."

CHAPTER XIII

Samantha stopped in her tracks. "Luke, my bill of sale! He's got my bill of sale!"

"So he has," Luke said shortly, getting a fresh grip on her arm and tugging her over to Sol and Mary. "You've got company, Sol."

"Company?" Both Sol and Mary looked around the terrace.

"Inside the house. The tinker," Samantha said breathlessly.

Mary crossed herself and Sol's jaw dropped. "How do you know?" he said, recovering.

"Somebody just made a hell of a clatter behind one of the windows," Luke said. "Who else could it be?"

Sol swallowed. "Kids?"

"Care to check it out?"

"No."

"Well, somebody'd better do something," Samantha said, the rainhat bobbing, "or he's going to get away."

"That's okay by me," Sol said. "Live and let—"

"But he's the one with my bill of sale," Samantha said.

Sol glanced at Mary, who looked as though something had come unstuck. "He's also too much for Riverford to handle right now," he said. "Isn't he, Mary?"

Mary sighed as one who had fought the good fight but knew when to quit. "Yes, it'd be best all around if he was allowed to get away."

"But my receipt!"

"There's something more to worry about than that, Samantha," Luke said and turned back to the others.

"He happens to know that she's not only got the diamonds listed on the paper he found but where they are. I don't think he should be wandering around with that information."

"Oh, boy," Sol said.

"How would he know that?" Mary asked.

Samantha impatiently waited while Luke explained, then she gave his arm a shake. "Come on, come on, do something before he gets away."

Sol scratched his chin. "Got any ideas?" he asked Luke.

"My second one is to send for help while we make sure he doesn't get away."

"What's your first one?"

"Get the hell out of Riverford."

"I kind of like that one. He's a mean feller."

Before Samantha could protest, Mary squared her shoulders and took charge. "Well, it's not possible to get out of Riverford, is it?" The lilt was gone again, the tone crisp and authoritative. "So then, I'll go after help and you three position yourselves where you'll be seeing him if he tries to get away. I'll be back in a jiffy."

"Oh, God, try to make it sooner," Luke said.

They found the tinker's entry on the far side of the house. Boards had been pulled off a window and lay in a heap on the rough stone decking. Sol went off to stand guard at a point where he could watch the front and the opposite side of the house, Samantha drew the southwest corner, while Luke hovered at the exposed window.

At her post Samantha brooded over the nearness of the bill of sale. Such as it was, it was the only thing she had to lend credence to her story. She stood around worrying about it for a moment or so and then went back to Luke. "What if he destroys my bill of sale?"

117

"It's probably destroyed already," he said, though not unkindly. "He was in the water, you know."

She hadn't thought of that. She considered it, then shook her head, the hat bobbing. "It could be dried," she said stubbornly and pulled at his arm, pleading, "Please, you've got to get it from him now."

"Now?"

"Yes, before he—"

He jerked free. "You think I'd go in there? Alone?"

"You mean you won't?"

"You're damn right I won't."

She couldn't believe it. She stared at him. She believed it. She wanted to kick him. Or cry. Or both. Instead she set her jaw. "Then, I will."

He picked up one of the boards. "Here, take this with you." He held out the nail-studded piece of wood.

"No, thanks," she said coldly.

"And what makes you think the guy's going to hand over the receipt without persuasion of sorts—if he still has it, that is."

She hadn't got that far in her thinking. "I'll—I'll offer him a reward."

"What makes you think he'll settle for a couple of bucks when he could grab a fortune with just a dip of the hand?"

She found the thought not as unsettling as it should have been. Getting proof of her innocence was uppermost in her mind, and if there was the slightest chance the tinker still had it, she wanted it in hand when Mr. Donegal arrived on the scene. "I'll tell him . . . I'll tell him . . . oh, I'll think of something. I want that receipt and I'm going in and get it."

"Okay, it's your blood. If you want to spill it, go ahead." He stood aside. "Because if you think he's going to wait and chat about a trade, you're crazy."

That she found unsettling. "He wouldn't do anything to me. Not with the police on the way."

"He's already facing a murder charge, don't forget."

That stopped her, but only for a moment. "Well, so am I and the key to my innocence is that bill of sale." She started to thrust a leg over the windowsill.

"Christ!" Luke grabbed her and pulled her back. "You'd really do it!"

"I would." She glared at him.

"You—you— Get out of my way," he ordered, shoving her aside.

"You don't have to—"

"Shut up." He got a grip on the nail-studded board.

"But you really don't, you know," she said, though she gave a sigh of relief that came from her toes.

"Okay, okay, you've made your point. You can remind me of it while they're sewing me up." He heaved himself over the sill and found her preparing to do the same. "Where the hell do you think you're going?"

"With you," she was surprised to hear herself say. She told herself it was because she was anxious to retrieve the receipt and had nothing to do with sticking close to him in case somebody had to yell for help.

"Oh, no, you're not. You stay with Sol until the others arrive. Then you get yourself and your goddamned diamonds in the middle of a lot of people and—"

"I'm either going in with you now or when you're out of sight. Make up your mind to that."

"Oh, my God," he moaned but he stood back and held out a helping hand. "I hope you're prepared to wind up with lumps on your head and none in your bosom," he said as she climbed in.

Once inside they stood still, getting their bearings. The bit of light from the window behind gave dim outline to shrouded furniture, massive in form. High ceilings were lost in shadow. Nooks and crannies became caverns of darkness. Samantha's determination was smothered in the hushed gloom of the long unused house. Perhaps they should wait until the others arrived, she thought, but Luke moved off before she could make the suggestion. Hurriedly she crept after him and grabbed a handful of his coat.

Startled, he spun around, board upraised. "That's a good way to get clobbered," he said in a hoarse whisper.

"I'm sorry," she whispered back.

He sniffed disbelievingly and suffered her hanging on to his arm as he resumed his way toward a pair of double doors at the far end of the large room. Any sound of their footsteps was swallowed up in the thick carpet.

The hinges of the tall heavy door grated as Luke pulled it open, and he swore softly but vehemently at the noise. He peered through the slight opening into the room beyond.

"Do you see him?" she whispered fearfully.

"Can't see a thing." He opened the door wider, and they cautiously moved into a large square entry hall. An unboarded fanlight over the huge double doors allowed enough of the overcast, drizzly morning to cast a ghostly light over the big room. Parquet showed faintly underfoot. There was a wide staircase at their left and enormous doors leading off on all sides.

Luke nodded at the double doors on the right. "Should lead to the room with the broken window," he whispered.

With each careful footstep they took across the parquet floor she thought less of the idea of sharing the big empty house with a suspected murderer, and by the time they reached the double doors, her mind was made up. Nothing would induce her to step into that room. She tugged on Luke's sleeve. "Luke—"

"Shshsh," he ordered, his hand on the great iron doorknob.

She jerked his sleeve. "But—"

"Quiet," he whispered hoarsely, turning the knob.

"No!" she hissed as he pushed in the door.

He turned to her in the half gloom. "No?"

"No. Let's get out of here."

"Good thinking." And at that moment voices calling their names came faintly to them. "Ah, the marines—"

He never finished the sentence. There was a sharp, quick grating of old hinges and a whooshing sound and Luke's arm pulled out of her grasp, and the next instant she felt herself yanked through the double doors and there was another whoosh and then pain smashed through her head and blackness roared up and swallowed her.

CHAPTER XIV

She opened her eyes. It was dark and cold, and her head was full of pain and buzzy noises. She rubbed her forehead. The buzzing swarmed. "Samantha?" It sounded like someone whispering through tissue paper. Warren? She stirred and felt the scratch of rough stone beneath her. Stone?

"Samantha?" The voice buzzed in her ear again. She reached for her bedside lamp and hit solid rock. Rock? "Where—" A hand shot out of the dark and clamped over her mouth.

"Shshsh," the voice whispered in her ear.

Her eyes flew open. Luke's voice! "Luke." The cry was muffled against his hand.

"Shshsh," he whispered again. "The tinker may be around. Are you all right?"

She nodded, which was a mistake. He took his hand away, and she lay there listening to the pain echo in her head while he stirred around at her side.

"I'm going to toss a coin and see if it raises Reilly," he whispered after a moment.

She clutched his arm. "What do we do if it does?"

"You crowd the wall. I'll probably bleed a lot."

She heard the coin clink some distance off, and when it stopped skidding along the stone flooring, she strained to hear the slightest sound, her nerve ends twitching with the thought of a murderer lurking in the pitch blackness.

And then at last Luke said softly, "Okay, I think we're alone."

" 'Think' doesn't put my mind at rest."

"Pretty sure, then I've been listening for sounds from him for a while and didn't hear any."

She gently eased herself to a sitting position. "My head's splitting," she groaned.

"There's a lot of that going around in here."

"Where do you suppose 'here' is and how long have we been in it?"

"I'd guess we're in that secret passageway Sol's so proud of, but I don't know how long we've been here. He stole our watches. He also got—"

Her hands flew to her chest. 32 A. "The diamonds!"

"The diamonds," he affirmed.

She sat still, expecting that the impact of the loss would hit her any second. Surely some cry of anguish was welling up in her inner depths. Warren's diamonds were gone, weren't they? So what? was what her inner depths came up with. The bill of sale was gone too, wasn't it? And the way things stood at the moment, without the bill of sale nobody was going to reap a harvest from any diamonds. Not if she was arrested before the real Amsterdam criminals were caught. And the way things were going, she wasn't too optimistic anymore about that happening. And if, God forbid, it did, with the third degree all Warren's part in the fiasco would be wormed out of her and a fat lot of good the diamonds would do for a political candidate involved in an international police action. His shiny image would erode in a hurry.

"You okay?" Luke's voice came out of the darkness.

Her head splitting, her bones aching, and a cold draft blowing on her, she said, "I'm in one piece but that's about all." Rebuttoning her jacket, she sniffed and searched her pockets for a handkerchief. Finding none, she explored the area around her for her handbag and made a further discovery. Her handbag was gone. "He got my handbag too."

"And my billfold. And our watches. The son of a bitch should've brought a shopping cart." He went on to make a few terse observations about life in general and then said, "Well, so that's that."

Her own reaction notwithstanding, Samantha felt he was passing over the theft of the diamonds rather lightly. "That's that? The diamonds are gone, and all you have to say is 'so that's that'?"

"No." There was a sound of stirring and moaning. Now his voice came from overhead. "I could add I'm damned glad to be alive."

She went limp as the full impact hit her. They had been in the hands of a murderer. "I'd like to get out of here," she said weakly.

"So would— Where the hell are my matches? Ah, here they are. So would I," he said and then started swearing again.

"What now?" she said sharply, almost afraid to ask.

"There's only one match left," he said disgustedly. "Well, let's see where we are."

The feeble light gave small comfort and no clue of the length of the narrow rock-walled passage with damp patches stealing down the sides. All it did was emphasize the Stygian darkness once it flickered out and increase Samantha's desire to quit the place. She was miserable with fear, cold, and most of all pain.

Gingerly she explored the back of her head. There was a huge lump but at least it wasn't split. Unless, she thought gloomily, she'd been unconscious long enough for it to have healed. She felt cold enough to have been lying there for days. "How long do you think we've been here?"

"I've no idea."

"Why don't we yell for help?"

"I figure if we can't hear anyone calling us, they won't hear us calling them."

"Maybe they gave up when we didn't answer. It wouldn't hurt to try."

"Go ahead if it'll make you feel better."

She gathered a lungful of air and gave a full-bodied but short-lived cry that sent every drop of blood pounding through her throbbing head.

"I'd rather you didn't do that again," Luke said in a strained voice.

"Oh, my head," she groaned.

"Make that two."

There were no answering cheers from the outside world. She drew her coat closer, running a hand over her newly flattened front. A thought struck her. "How did you know the diamonds were gone?"

"There was nothing to do while I waited for you to come to so I thought I'd take inventory. Good thing too. You were fair game for pneumonia the way he left you. I . . . uh . . . straightened things for you."

"Nice of you."

"It was nothing."

She thought about that. Probably didn't mean anything. She sat listening to his shuffling footsteps, strangely comforted by the sound, and found herself wondering how Warren would behave in such circumstances. Probably be sitting in her spot and listening to her shuffling footsteps was the first thing that came to mind.

Immediately she was ashamed of the thought. Warren was a man of ideas. Not action. Poor Warren. His big idea had certainly laid an egg. No diamonds. No Honorable whatever. No governor's mansion. No White House.

She tried to feel the grief she felt she should feel but found herself more concerned with the loss of her handbag. Everything in it had more meaning to her than the diamonds. Suddenly she was aware of complete silence. "Luke!" she said, frightened.

"What?"

Relief filled her. "What're you doing?"

"Trying to decide if I've turned around."

"I hope you come across my purse."

"I have a feeling it's going to brighten some female tinker's day."

"Don't say that. My passport's in it."

"Try to look on the bright side. You're not going anywhere at the moment." His voice was moving away. "Keep talking so I can keep my bearings."

"And you keep talking so I know you haven't gone off without me."

"Why should I do that? Being with you is a thrill a minute."

He shuffled off, and she mulled over his words. He had a right to be bitter. She'd brought him nothing but trouble. He probably wouldn't ever want to see her again—if they ever got out of this mess, that is.

"Samantha?"

"What?"

"Talk."

"I'm sorry I got you into this mess."

There was no response, and she waited a moment longer. "Luke?"

"What?"

"I said I was sorry I got you into this mess."

"I heard you."

"Oh." She drew her collar tighter and brushed away wisps of hair blowing around her face. "Luke."

"What?" His voice came from some distance away.

Please say it's all right? Not Luke. He wouldn't say anything just because it was the expected thing. Warren always did. Warren. She tried to call up a clear picture of him, then gave up. She sat huddled, listening to

126

Luke's footsteps carefully scraping along the stone. It suddenly occurred to her she knew very little about him. He could even be married.

"Luke, are you married?"

"No."

She found herself pleased he wasn't married and she wondered about that. Rather silly, really. What difference did it make? "Are you engaged?"

"No, I'm not engaged," he said in a preoccupied voice.

"Or anything?"

"Anything? What anything?" His footsteps were returning.

"Do you live with anyone?"

"Yes indeed, every chance I get."

That didn't surprise her either. Now you see him, now you don't was exactly how she'd pegged him. Though, again, what difference did it make? He still wouldn't want to see her again, ties or no ties. "I don't suppose you'd ever want to see me again if we ever get out of this mess."

"Well, now, I don't know. What did you have in mind? A cozy little threesome of you and Warren and me?" His voice grew closer.

"No, of course not. I meant—" She wasn't sure what she meant.

"If you're interested in starting something," he said from directly overhead, "you've chosen a hell of a spot but—"

"You told me to talk," she said quickly. "And that's all I'm doing. Making conversation." Of course she was. "I'm only interested in getting out of here."

"Ah, well." She sensed amusement in his voice, then it became brisk. "Well, there's no way out that I could find in that direction. Not unless it's one of those knock-three-times-on-the-fourth-stone affairs."

Strands of hair drifted into her eyes, and she brushed them away and shifted her position. "What are we going to do?"

"You really ask me that quite a lot, you know."

"I guess I do." She thought about that. "So what are we going to do?"

"*I'm* going to check the other direction. And *you* pull in your feet. I've got enough bruises for one day."

"Can't I go with you? It's so cold down here. There's a draft blowing—"

"A draft? You feel a draft?"

"Yes, and it's—" She broke off, aware he had dropped down beside her. "What—?" His face brushed hers.

"By God, there is a draft!" he said and hugged her. "Come on!"

She was no longer cold and rather liked it where she was. But then he released her and began tugging her to her feet.

"Come on, come on," he said. "Where there's a draft, there's got to be an opening. And watch your head. The ceiling is low in places."

They got under way, Samantha hanging on to his sleeve, her head thumping. Cobwebs floated onto her face, and she tried not to think of leggy things dropping down or furry things crawling around her feet.

It seemed to her that they'd gone miles when Luke stumbled. He swore and threw out an arm, halting her. "Watch it, there's a break in the flooring here. All we need now is a twisted ankle to add to the excitement."

She felt around and found a wide separation in the stone. "I found it," she said and cautiously negotiated her way around it so as not to rock their relationship any further. He got under way again and she grabbed his coat. They shuffled along through the pitch black, and a few steps later her foot nudged something. She let go of his coat and froze. A body? For a horrified instant she expected a hand to wrap around her ankle. When nothing happened, she pushed her foot against the object and it slid. Her handbag? "Luke, wait. I've kicked something," she said, dropping to the floor.

Immediately she felt him down beside her, and their hands touched the object at the same moment. It was a pouch. It jerked out of her grasp. "Luke, it's one of the pouches." She held out her hands. "Where is it?" In a moment she felt the soft flannel envelope and the small hard lumps through their thick wadding. "It *is* one of the pouches!" she said.

"And the stones are still in it," Luke said. "Here, give it to me. I'll keep it for you."

The pouch was pulled out of her hand again.

"The bastard must've tripped and dropped it," Luke said, moving away. "Come on, that draft's really blowing. And from straight ahead."

She grabbed his receding coat, giving a passing thought to his having assumed possession of the diamonds. But then she too felt the increased force of the draft, and her relief at the thought of escape from that awful place drove the question from her mind.

Once more they moved along the black passageway, carefully but steadily, until suddenly he stopped and she ran into him.

"Christ, it's a dead end," he said.

"But I feel air," she cried. She moved around him and frantically ran her fingers along slabs of rock, breaking nails but not caring. She found the opening. It was a narrow slit between rocks. About waist high. "Luke, I found it!"

His hands found hers, and they crowded each other, searching out the break. His fell away. "About all it's good for is air," he said bitterly. "At least we won't suffocate."

Was he giving up? Scenes of whitened bones found in sealed passageways flashed before her eyes. "But there's got to be a way out! Reilly got out."

"Well, I don't happen to have Reilly's inside information," he snapped. "I'm just a poor slob passing through this cockamamy place with its trees in the middle of roads. Because fairies live in them. Of all the goddamned things."

"But—" She bit back asking what they were going to do now, sensing it might get her a smack in the teeth, considering the way he was swearing and banging the wall.

For lack of something better to do while he enlarged on his theme, she tried pushing and prodding the patch of wall nearest her. Finding a wedgelike piece of rock projecting from the others, she gave it a shove. The wall swung open.

Luke broke off midword. There was a moment of awed silence. Then he said, "How the hell did you do that?"

She found her voice. "I've connections in a tree outside of town."

Actually the entire wall hadn't swung open—just about a three-foot square of it at waist level. And it hadn't exactly swung open. It had merely groaned and scraped along a few inches or so. Luke gave it a hefty shove. Daylight, a patch of glorious daylight, spilled into the passageway.

Samantha took a deep breath of fresh air.

Luke turned to her with a look of wholehearted approval. "Nice work," he said. "A half hour or so sealed in a passage will never get us on talk shows, but personally I think it's long enough."

Only half an hour? As far back as she could remember they'd been stuck in the creepy place. "Is that all we've been in here?"

"More or less, I'd say." He hoisted himself up and crawled out on his stomach. Once out, he turned and offered his hand. A moment later she joined him.

The south of France on its best day couldn't have looked better to her than that blustery Irish countryside did at that moment. Knee-deep in the tangle of long grass, they stood grinning and looking around.

They had come out beneath the terrace on the opposite side from where they had entered the house.

A lot had been going on during their confinement, and Samantha guessed they'd been in the passageway longer than Luke had thought. Boards had been pulled away from most of the windows and doors, and from inside there came the sounds of pounding and thumping and voices calling back and forth.

Luke seemed in no hurry to announce their return to the outside world. Samantha was glad. Not simply because she dreaded going back to the trials and tribulations life had suddenly thrown at her, but because she was strangely reluctant to break the tenuous bond their shared danger had forged. She was sure it would snap the minute they got back among those same trials and tribulations.

She drew another deep breath of the sweet fresh air and, still grinning, looked up at Luke. He grinned down at her and, putting an arm around her shoulder, gave her a little hug. "You were real brave back in there, Mary Samantha Malooly," he said.

"I was, wasn't I," she said, liking the honest admiration in his voice and the light in his eyes.

"You were indeed," he said.

They both laughed and he hugged her again. They stood a moment longer chuckling happily and looking at each other. Then the mirth gradually faded from his eyes, and a new light came into them, deeper and softer, and they held hers in a long unbroken look. She felt she was at a turning point. She had only to take one small step and things would never be the same for her again.

And then somebody yelled, "It's them, it's them! Glory be! They've escaped the murderer!"

Luke's arm fell away, he stepped back, and the moment was gone. There was no time for Samantha to reflect on whether she'd have taken that step or not, for instantly heads popped out of windows and doors flew open. The next moment they were plunged into the real world and people were scrambling around them on all sides—more people than Samantha cared to see.

There were also two she was not aware of.

A few hundred feet down in the overgrown hedge, Reilly watched. And just a short distance away from him, crouched in a copse of cypress and hidden by the long grasses growing around it, Coffey watched as well—watched and listened.

CHAPTER XV

Sol leaped down the steps with Mary at his heels. She patted, and crooned over Luke's and Samantha's injuries while an assortment of Irishmen in baggy trousers, coats, and cloth caps fought the five O'Callaghan Brothers for position.

Everyone talked at once thanking the Lord, praising the saints, and peppering Luke with questions, until Mr. Donegal and Hugh elbowed their way through. Mr. Donegal silenced them all with a wag of a bushy eyebrow.

Samantha quickly slid behind Luke, suddenly aware that she'd lost her hat and glasses somewhere along the way.

Mr. Donegal asked Luke what had happened, and when Luke finished his hazy version, Mr. Donegal's expression was guarded, his tone, careful. "And could you be describing the man?"

"No, I never saw who or what hit me."

"Mrs. Carter?"

"No, no, I didn't see him either," she said quickly over Luke's shoulder.

Mr. Donegal's face cleared. "So you're neither one knowing who it might have been."

"Oh, I've got a pretty good idea who it was," Luke said. "That tinker I found on the beach this morning, I think."

There was a slight stir among the natives. Mr. Donegal gave Luke a bland face. "Now, I'm remembering you were telling me that one was dead."

"I was wrong. He must've been wounded. Wounded and unconscious, that's all."

133

"And you're saying despite his wounds he made his way all the way here?"

"I've got a pretty good idea about that too. Want to hear it?"

There was more stirring and some shuffling in the ranks.

"I'll be hearing your theories some other time," Mr. Donegal said, unruffled. "Do you mind now I'm wondering just why you went inside? And taking your wife with you?"

"Yes, well, we thought he was hurt, you know."

"Ah, yes. You have this need to rescue, don't you? Now 'tis more puzzling why the man didn't remain hidden in the passageway, him being that certain we'd no idea where it was. Why would he make his presence known?"

There was a murmur of "aye, aye" all around.

"Robbery, what else?" Luke said. He winced at the jab Samantha gave him in the back. "He got our watches and my billfold and—uh—Samantha's handbag."

Mr. Donegal was not satisfied. "It would hardly seem worth the risk."

Luke waved an impatient hand. "Shouldn't we be looking for him instead of standing around chatting? He could be hiding in the grounds, you know."

Samantha started, looking fearfully around. She'd like the rest of the diamonds back for Warren's sake but not under Mr. Donegal's eyes. She jabbed Luke again and he turned with the look of a man who'd had about enough for one morning. "Yes?"

"I . . . uh. . . ." All eyes turned to her and she ducked behind a hand, rubbing her forehead. "I . . ."

His expression softened slightly. He patted her shoulder and said to Mr. Donegal, "Samantha's had a trying morning. Can we—"

Mr. Donegal showed sudden concern. "Ah, and I was forgetting! To be sure. You both go along with him," he said, pointing his thumb at Sol. "I'm thinking she should be lying down. Such an experience cannot have been good for her at a time like this."

"A time like this?" Luke asked.

Samantha wondered about that too.

"Sol was telling me last night about Mrs. Carter's condition."

"Oh?"

Both Luke and Samantha looked to Sol. He grinned feebly.

Mr. Donegal waved his Greek chorus toward the house. "We'll be looking around here further and will come by later if there's anything to report."

Luke sourly watched him herd his band of Irishmen back into the house. "Why the hell are they checking inside again? Why not the grounds? Though I suppose it doesn't matter. Reilly's probably halfway across the country by now. With Samantha's diamonds."

There was a rustle in the cypress copse that no one noticed, it having been drowned out by Mary's sorrowful little cry. "He got the diamonds?"

"One pouch, anyway. Dropped the other. We found it in the passage." Luke pulled the pouch from his pocket.

The cypress rustled again, unnoticed.

"Put it away, put it away," Samantha said, darting a look at the opened windows and doors. "Please, can't we leave now?"

As they were climbing into the Donegal car, Luke paused to look back. "On second thought maybe we'd better hope Reilly got away. If he were caught with the diamonds on him—"

"But the bill of sale," Mary said. "He's got the bill of sale—"

"After all the time he spent in the water, I don't see how it could be anything but pulp now," Sol said.

Samantha avoided Luke's I-told-you-so look as Mary set the car into motion.

"Just why *did* you go inside the house?" Sol asked.

Luke leaned back and closed his eyes. "I haven't figured that one out yet."

No one spoke on the short drive back to the cottage. Samantha stared out the window at the rain-spattered thorn bushes, resolutely emptying her mind of everything but the prospect of stretching out with a cold cloth on her head.

She announced this intention as they filed into the cottage. "And I don't care to talk with anyone for the next ten years."

"I'll bring you a lunch tray," Mary said.

"No, thank you. I don't want anything."

"At least have a cup of—"

"Don't say it, Mary. Please," Luke said. "What she needs is a good stiff belt of Scotch. So lie down, Samantha. I'll bring it in to you."

She would have liked that, but she had no sooner stretched out than she fell into the deep sleep of the emotionally exhausted. Luke looked down at her a few minutes later with bemused compassion. He drew the comforter over her and set the glass of Scotch down on the night table.

Returning a half hour later with a drink of his own, Luke gently roused her. He retrieved her drink from the night table and held it out to her. "Here, take a good slug."

There was something about his expression. "Why?" she asked.

"There's something you ought to be prepared for."

"I don't want to hear it." She pulled the cloth down over her eyes and fell back on the pillow.

"Samantha."

"What?"

"We've been listening to the news."

She raised a corner of the cloth. "Do you have to tell me now? I was just drifting off to sleep."

"You've been asleep for half an hour." He removed the cloth and brushed hair from her forehead. "And I think you ought to know what's been happening in case Mr. Donegal gets onto it and trots around." He shoved the drink at her again, but she shook her head. She had a hunch she was going to need her wits in first-class working order.

He considered the two glasses briefly, then downed both of them, put the glasses on the table, and seated himself on the edge of the bed. "Some of the people who were on the flight from Amsterdam have contacted the police. A bird-watching woman from Manchester and two priests from Cork. Remember them?"

She sighed deeply and nodded.

"All three are working with sketch artists to produce your likeness for the newspaper and TV."

"Oh boy," she groaned, and looked regretfully at her empty liquor glass.

"There's more."

She moaned.

"Your friends at Parknasilla are more concerned about you than you think. They got worried and got in touch with New York and they've got the police looking for you." He took a deep breath. "According to the radio they're sending out Wirephotos."

"Bingo."

"Bingo. Wirephotos of the missing Samantha Malloy side by side with sketches of the fugitive Mary Samantha Malooly—"

"Police'll be falling all over themselves, trying to get to Parknasilla first," Samantha said.

"With Mr. Donegal, little old Johnny-on-the-spot."

She threw the comforter off, swung her legs onto the floor, and sat hunched, pulling her misery around her like a blanket.

"No 'Do something'?" Luke said when she continued to sit in glum silence.

"There's only one thing to do. Tell Mr. Donegal everything."

"Now you're talking."

"What do you think they'll do to me?"

"I don't know. Take you back to Amsterdam, I guess."

"To prison," she said with the dull certainty of one who's as good as in jail.

"I doubt it, once you've told your story and what's-his-name, Warren, backs it up."

Warren back her up? She thought of his single-minded pursuit of that first step up the political ladder and knew without a doubt that he would never voluntarily back her up. Before he'd sacrifice his career, he'd sacrifice her, reluctantly perhaps but without hesitation. And it naturally followed that even if the real criminals were caught this very minute the worldwide hoopla surrounding her failure to show at Parknasilla and her brush with the police wiped out their future together. But that didn't matter. She paused and reflected on that. It was sad but true. Sad because the death of a relationship deserved at least a moment's sense of loss. She was just sorry that her carelessness was going to ruin his carefully nurtured plans. Luke had been right after all. If she'd put the bill of sale in her passport folder where important papers belonged, she wouldn't need Warren's testimony to support the legitimacy of her being at Mijnheer VanDam's or her legal right to the diamonds in her possession. In all fairness she owed it to Warren to keep him out of the picture as long as possible in the hope that the crime would be solved before his testimony was needed.

But there was no point in telling Luke that. He might not understand her reasoning. She wasn't all that sure she understood it herself, considering all Warren had to face was a political setback while she was going to jail for robbery and murder. But there it was. She sighed. She was sick of the whole mess.

"In a way," she said to Luke, "I'll be glad to get this business over with. Being a fugitive is exhausting." She sighed again. "But then it's not easy to adjust to the idea of being a convict either." She began nibbling on a thumbnail.

Luke reached over and took her hand away from her mouth and laid it on his palm, straightening the long slender fingers. "Well, I can't see any lawman in his right mind believing you could pull off a quarter-of-a-million-dollar diamond heist let alone risk breaking one of these fingernails murdering your victim."

She found his holding her hand more comforting than his words. "I hope you're right," she said gloomily.

His arm slid around her. "Don't worry, Samantha. As soon as the phones work, I'll get in touch with an international law firm I know and find out the procedure to keep you out of jail. I'll work it all out."

His arm felt good too. She relaxed a little. Just a little. "I don't have much faith in those phones working."

He drew her closer. "Think of it this way. If they don't, Donegal can't get in touch with the outside world either."

That and the circle of his arms comforted her. She suddenly realized that the moment they had emerged from the tunnel and he had held her in his arms had been a turning point for her. That was when Warren had ceased to matter. And Luke did. And if she was smart, she'd slip out from under his arm before he mattered too much and she got involved in a whole new problem. Because Luke Carter was just filling in time the best way he knew. Hadn't he freely admitted he got involved with women every chance he got? A woman looking for anything lasting was looking at the wrong man. She knew that, didn't she? So she laid her head on his shoulder. And his other arm came around her and she sighed and his arms tightened.

She could smell the Scotch on his breath so she knew he was looking down at her. And she knew if she looked up he was going to kiss her and there was just no way things were going to stop there. So she looked up. And he lowered his head. And there was a gentle rapping at the door.

"Son of a bitch," Luke said an inch away from her mouth.

Saved, saved in the nick of time, she told herself. But she heard herself say, "Ah well . . ." and she closed the gap. And it was wonderful. Long and deep and tasting of Scotch and birds-singing-bells-ringing wonderful. But the rapping became more anxious.

Finally Luke raised his head and glared over at the noise. He brushed her lips with his, said, "Don't move," and went to the door.

It was Sol. He shot Samantha a weak smile and then said something in quick undertones to Luke.

"Christ!" Luke said. "Okay, we'll be right there."

She knew the spell was broken.

Gathering herself together as he closed the door, she frowned deeply. "What now?" she asked.

"Donegal's here. He stopped back at O'Sullivan House after lunch for another look around and found Reilly's body."

She sighed deeply and brushed the hair off her forehead. Back to reality with a thud. "So what else is new?" she said.

CHAPTER XVI

Luke moved away from the door. "Donegal wants to ask us some questions."

Samantha regarded him bleakly. There was no caress in his eyes. There was no tremble in his voice. Most likely there never had been. Most likely, she told herself, she'd been under the influence of his Scotch. She got up and dragged herself over to the mirror and started combing what was left of her hair. "I'll bet he does. Like 'Where did the tinker get these diamonds, do you suppose?' and 'Whatever is this wad of paper?' It, of course, being my bill of sale."

"Well, go tell him and get it over with."

"You say that so easily. But then you're not the one headed for jail. Or are you? As accessory after the fact."

He met her eyes in the mirror. "That depends entirely on you."

She put the comb down and turned around without a final glance at herself. A first. "On me?"

"It's up to you whether Mary and Sol and I get involved."

"But you're already involved."

"We could be just innocent bystanders who thought we were protecting you from some domestic problem."

She stared at him. He'd had it all figured out. Oh, yes, the spell was broken. "And why do you think he'll believe that?"

"With the shenanigans he's pulling around here, he's in no position to give us any trouble if he doesn't."

She thought about that. "Then maybe he can't give me any trouble either."

"Maybe *he* can't but half the hemisphere is looking for you and headed this way, remember? No, Samantha, your best bet is to put yourself in Mr. Donegal's custody. You'll be all right, I promise you."

It was hard to put much faith in the promise of a man who kisses you one minute and throws you to the wolves the next. But all she said was, "That's easy enough for an innocent bystander to say."

He gave her a quick speculative look. "Samantha, don't think that I'm deserting you."

"Hah," she said dismally.

"Nothing of the sort. It's just that I've got a hell of a lot riding on this bid on the coast and even more at stake if the job in the Middle East doesn't wind up on schedule. I'll be back with you as soon as I get things organized, believe me. And in the meantime I've got a whole battery of attorneys I'll put to handling your case."

She thought of the attorney she already had, Warren, sitting back in New York in wall-to-wall isolation, surrounded by his rosy dreams and shadowy schemes. She decided she didn't have much faith in attorneys either. "Thanks, but I'm hoping things don't get that far."

He considered her briefly, then said, "Well, let's go face Donegal."

"Might as well," she said and led the way down the hallway. Just outside the kitchen she stopped, her mind's eye seeing ABANDON ALL HOPE cut above the doorway. Then Luke gave her a little nudge, and she prepared to face the enemy.

Mr. Donegal, Mary, and Sol were sitting at the kitchen table. Sol rose and pulled out a chair for Samantha, and Mary reached for the teapot. Plates of cheese and cold meat were barely touched.

Mary poured a cup for Samantha. "You've heard?

142

Father and Hugh found Reilly's body," she said solemnly.

Samantha nodded and, not caring to meet Mr. Donegal's eyes, started piling food onto a plate. The prisoner would eat a hearty luncheon.

" 'Tis glad I am to see you've an appetitie," Mr. Donegal said. "You're feeling all right, then, are you?"

"Yes," she said warily, nervously applying herself to the food on her plate. What was this? Some kind of Irish flimflam to catch her off guard?

"Ah, I'm that glad." Mr. Donegal eyed Luke with disapproval. "You should not have allowed her to go inside O'Sullivan House with you, risking danger to herself and the baby."

Samantha's fork halted midair.

"Baby?" Luke said.

"Sol's told me, you know, that you're expecting."

"It sort of slipped out last night," Sol said weakly.

"Oh, it did, did it?" Luke cleared his throat. "Mr. Donegal, there's something—"

"It's no matter now," Mr. Donegal said, closing the subject with a wave of the hand. "Now then, you've said Reilly took some things from you . . ."

Samantha took her gaze from Sol and braced herself. This was it!

". . . but we found nothing on him," Mr. Donegal continued.

Luke's mouth fell open. "Nothing?" he said, recovering.

"Nothing."

Samantha shot a glance at Luke. What had happened to the diamonds now? An ugly thought crossed her mind. Luke? Could he have—No. Ridiculous. Or was it? He could have found Reilly's body during his first search of the passageway, helped himself to the dia-

143

monds, and while doing so inadvertently dropped one pouch. No, that wouldn't work. They'd been going in the opposite direction when they'd stumbled over the pouch. But still . . . he'd taken possession of it, hadn't he? And he had said he was worried about money matters. She drew a shaky breath. Had he killed . . . while she was unconscious . . . had he . . . ? She couldn't bring herself to form the thought. But where were the diamonds?

Mr. Donegal produced his notebook. "Now if you'll be describing the things you're missing."

"Well . . . money . . . traveler's checks, that sort of thing," Luke said.

"Jewelry?"

Samantha stiffened.

Luke encouraged her with a nod.

She opened her mouth and shoved in a forkful of food. She simply could not say the fatal words.

"Well?" Mr. Donegal said.

Luke glanced away from her, disgusted. "We told you our watches were taken."

"You're not missing any jewelry along with the watches, Mrs. Carter?"

Here we go, Samantha told herself. It had been a trap all along. "Jewelry?" she said faintly, stalling.

"I was noticing you're not wearing your wedding ring."

She slid a glance at Luke. His expression announced, Now dammit, is the time to tell all. She gathered herself. "I . . . you see . . . I . . . uh . . . don't wear jewelry while traveling." She shoved a forkful of meat into her mouth and began chewing rapidly.

" 'Tis probably a good idea," Mr. Donegal conceded. "Well now, we'll be looking further for your valuables, you can be sure." He closed his notebook.

"I'm not counting a lot on getting them back," Luke said, obviously disappointed in the whole human race.

"And why is that?" Mr. Donegal asked mildly enough.

"Because Riverford seems to be a haven for criminals."

Samantha shriveled within herself, taking Luke's words personally.

So did Mr. Donegal. "Perhaps to an outsider, Mr. Carter, our methods of dealing with crime may seem a bit strange—"

"That's putting it in a nutshell. One doesn't often come across the to-hell-with-the-victim school of detection."

"On the contrary, young man, we are vitally concerned with victims."

"You'd have a hell of a time convincing me of that," Luke said. "I saw your methods in action a couple of times today, remember. Particularly when you had Reilly's body shoved under a hedge thinking him dead at the time. Not even giving a thought to a decent burial for the poor slob."

Samantha winced. If there was a wrong way to rub Mr. Donegal, Luke was bound to take it. She stole a look at Mr. Donegal, expecting to find smoke coming out of his nostrils, but oddly enough he hadn't turned a hair at Luke's bluntness.

"That was a temporary action till Father Shea arrived to provide the proper ceremonies," Mr. Donegal said with a dismissing wave.

Luke snorted.

Then Mr. Donegal leaned toward him. "Now, Mr. Carter, speaking of Reilly as we more recently found him brings me to the matter I wished to discuss with you. Did you kill him?"

Samantha dropped her fork. The clatter went unheeded in the wake of the shock wave that swept the table. Both Sol's and Mary's jaws had dropped. Luke was staring at Mr. Donegal as though he'd taken a blow across the windpipe.

Samantha's stomach turned over. Why had Mr. Donegal asked that? Had he found some evidence? She felt as though the blood had left her body and returned with a rush. It pounded in her ears. Her doubts came back with a rush. Had Luke—She made herself finish the thought. Had Luke killed Reilly? For the diamonds? She forced herself to face the facts. It would've been easy for a man as big and fit as Luke to quickly overpower a weakened, wounded assailant, even in the pitch dark. He could have done so and hidden the body while she was still unconscious. There had been that period of silence before she'd called out, anxious because she couldn't hear his shuffling. He'd said he was searching the passageway for a way out. He could actually have been checking to make sure Reilly was out of the way of her feet when they got on the move, couldn't he? Her thoughts flew back and forth. There was always the memory he'd said he had money problems. And he hadn't been all that concerned when she first discovered the diamonds had been taken from her bra, had he? And he had abruptly assumed possession of the recovered pouch, hadn't he? She very much wanted to cry. Luke, Luke. *I can't . . . I won't believe it,* she told herself miserably. She looked at him again.

He was still staring at Mr. Donegal. "I'll be goddamned," he said, apparently finding his voice at last. "You can't be serious."

"Well now, you were the last to see Reilly alive."

"I didn't even see him," he roared. "The bastard hit me from behind and I went out like a light."

Mr. Donegal turned to Samantha. "And this is so, Mrs. Carter?"

"Yes," she said in a small voice.

He leaned forward. "I'll be asking you to think carefully, Mrs. Carter. You're knowing Mr. Carter was unconscious?"

"I—I . . . heard something hit something. And then I was knocked unconscious too." Somehow she managed to get the words past the restriction in her throat.

Mr. Donegal leaned back, a pleased expression on his face. "Then you did not actually witness your husband's unconsciousness."

No she hadn't, had she? All she remembered was a sound and Luke's arm pulling away. Misery filled her. "No . . . no I didn't . . . really."

Luke reared his head like a bull moose ready to do battle. "What the hell reason would I have to do the guy in?"

Samantha could think of fifty thousand of them. She searched his face.

"Self-defense would be a sound reason, Mr. Carter."

Luke considered Mr. Donegal for a long moment. Then he nodded grimly and looked levelly at him. Samantha knew there was a perfectly sound reason about to be flung back in Mr. Donegal's teeth.

"I see," Luke said. "It'd make things a lot healthier around Riverford, wouldn't it, if this job could be pinned on some tourist. One protecting his . . . uh . . . pregnant wife, for instance." He shot an angry eye at Samantha. "Well, let me tell you, Mr. Donegal, I'm not going to be the patsy for anybody. In the first place—"

Samantha could see it coming and everything fled from her mind except self-preservation. She broke in, "In the first place we searched the passageway and there was no Reilly in there."

147

"Did you—" Mr. Donegal began when Luke cut him short.

"Just a minute, Mr. Donegal. Just where did you find the body anyway?" he said with a fine-honed edge to his voice.

Mr. Donegal spent a long moment studying his ball-point pen. Finally, with great reluctance, he said, "In the entrance hall."

"The entrance hall!" Luke bellowed. "And you didn't notice a body in the entrance hall until you went back after lunch? That whole gaggle of people looking for us this morning, what were they doing, for Christ's sake? Climbing over and around the guy?"

Mr. Donegal gave a large sigh and threw down his pen. "No, Mr. Carter, we're of a mind the tinker Coffey killed Reilly after we left."

Birds burst into song in Samantha's heart. "Thank God," she said. Luke was innocent. And that meant Coffey had the diamonds. Luke was doubly innocent. "Oh, thank God."

Luke took his attention away from Mr. Donegal long enough to give her a look that tabled her relief for further study. Then he turned back to Mr. Donegal. "So why all this footsying around trying to make me the goat?" he demanded.

"As you said. It'd make things easier if the tinkers think you accidentally killed Reilly while protecting your wife. It'll be bad enough with the Reillys milling about, wailing over the body and thieving but 'tis better than having the two clans fighting and killing in revenge on our doorsteps." He gave an even deeper sigh and settled his gaze on Luke. "Mr. Carter, I'm asking if you'll be assuming the blame."

"Not a chance," Luke said firmly. "My immediate plans don't include being thrown in jail and tried for murder."

Lucky you, Samantha thought bitterly.

"Oh, don't worry about that," Sol said, leaving no doubt whose side he was on. "There'd be no formal legal procedure. We don't even have a jail, remember? Just a sort of lean-to behind the Emporium."

"And of course," Mary put in eagerly, "you'd certainly not be confined in that. For one thing it's where we've put the corpse." She crossed herself.

The reminder that Riverford had no jail didn't comfort Samantha. Things could change in a moment, she reflected gloomily, if a bunch of warring tinkers brought outside police parachuting into Riverford with someone higher in command and more on top of things than Mr. Donegal. There was only one solution.

"Luke," she said, "you've got to help these people. Say that you killed the tinker."

He took his time in turning to her. "I beg your pardon?"

"Do as Mr. Donegal asked. Please."

She could tell by his cold expression that he thought poorly of the idea.

Not Mr. Donegal. He beamed his approval. " 'Tis true as we've said. There'd be no trial. 'Twould merely be an informal hearing around the council table to satisfy the Reilly clan that there'd been an accident during the course of self-defense."

"And supposing it doesn't satisfy them?"

"I'm thinking it will."

"Well, thinking isn't good enough. It's my neck that's sticking out. These tinkers have a nasty habit of taking matters into their own hands."

"Only in dealing out justice among their own kind," Mr. Donegal said. "They'd not be anxious to become involved with courts of law. Particularly when the deceased had broken into private property and attacked innocent bystanders. One being a pregnant woman."

149

"You don't want blood running down the streets of Riverford, do you?" Samantha said hastily, throwing in a red herring.

"I'm less keen about seeing the sight of my own blood."

"There's really nothing to worry about," Sol said.

"Then you take the honors."

"He can't," Mr. Donegal said regretfully. "It's the protecting of your pregnant wife that will have the Reilly's accepting their clansman's fate."

"Now about that—"

"You'd be a hero to the whole of Riverford," Mr. Donegal said.

"We'd say Masses for your intentions," Mary said.

"What a story to tell our child!" Samantha said.

"Oh, my God!" Luke said.

Samantha shriveled under his stare. Now she'd done it. What had made her say a thing like that? He looked as though he'd like to push her off a cliff. Would he push her into jail instead?

Then he tore his gaze away from her and slammed his fist down on the table. "Look! Forget it! Find yourself another pigeon, Mr. Donegal. Or better yet, why don't you do what you had in mind this morning? Quietly bury the guy, and nobody'll be the wiser."

Mr. Donegal's round rosy face got rosier and he threw Luke a steely eye. "That's a terrible accusation, young man."

"Come now, Mr. Donegal, I'm not stupid. And it'd save a heap of trouble. Besides, I was wrong about it's not being a decent burial. I didn't know you had a priest to do it up right."

Mr. Donegal struggled with some inner turmoil. Finally he sighed. " 'Tis too late for that. Father Shea returned to his village and there's none now to give a Christian burying."

Luke frowned. "How could he return to his village? The bridges are out."

"Why, by rowing to the other side of course."

Rowing to the other side. Samantha slumped. My God, why hadn't they thought of that? She looked at Luke.

His mouth was open and he was sitting in stunned silence. Then he said in a strangled voice, "Do you mean to tell me I could've got out of here this morning?"

"You could've if you'd had a boat."

Luke gathered steam. "Well, by God I'll get a boat!"

Samantha's heart seemed to stop. He was leaving her.

"It'll not be that easy, I'm thinking," Mr. Donegal said.

"What about the boat the priest took?"

Oh, he was leaving her all right.

"But it's on the other side now," Mr. Donegal pointed out.

"Well then, damnit, how about those O'Callaghan Brothers? Or anyone else who has a boat? I'll pay anything they want."

Mr. Donegal got to his feet. "Those who have boats are worrying about the tinker's murder just now." He looked around, found his black hat, and flicked an imaginary speck off the brim. "I've a mind they'll feel more like doing business after the hearing."

"That's blackmail," Luke said.

"You might say so. We're thinking it's self-preservation." He put on his hat as though it were a laurel wreath. "Ah, well, I'll just be letting you think it over."

CHAPTER XVII

The sound of Mr. Donegal's car faded. Luke sat staring into the distance. Mary drank tea. Sol made little mounds of bread crumbs. Samantha ate and brooded over the thought that Luke would go off and leave her. The fire hissed in the grate; water dripped off the thatched roof; a fresh breeze sent a shutter gently knocking.

At length Luke shifted in his chair and cleared his throat. Samantha stopped chewing. Mary stopped sipping. Sol stopped making little mounds of bread crumbs.

"You know," Luke said to no one in particular, "I didn't even have to come to Ireland. There were a couple of other jobs I could've gone after. One in Africa. And a good one in South America. I just thought Ireland would be a nice change after the desert. An easy flight to London or Paris for a holiday or else stick around and fish. I heard the fishing was good here."

"Oh, it is. It is," Mary said.

"Salmon and trout're both very good. Particularly at this time of year," Sol said.

"You forgot suckers," Luke said. He got up and walked around the room, his hands shoved in his pockets. Probably to keep from punching somebody in the mouth, Samantha thought and went back to chewing. Mary and Sol looked at each other and then away. Mary resumed sipping and Sol smashed his little mounds of bread crumbs. He cringed a little as Luke came back and stood over him.

"You might have told me this morning about the priest rowing across the river."

"I thought he'd left yesterday after the baptism."

"It's damned funny. Here I've been trying to get out of Riverford all day with no luck, and other people have been wandering in and out whenever they feel like it. The priest, Reilly, Reilly's daughter, that guy who got Reilly. And by the way, did anybody look for him? Or was it just agreed all around to go after me?"

Sol squirmed. "They looked."

"But not very hard, is that it?"

"They searched the grounds. And inside the house," Mary said defensively.

"Inside the house? Now why would they expect a murderer to hang around inside the house?"

"They were looking for the secret passage," Mary said. "They thought he might be hiding in it."

"Looking for the passage? All they had to do was go in from the outside—" Luke's eyebrows climbed up his forehead. "Don't tell me somebody closed that block of stone." He came around the table.

Sol and Mary looked away.

"Somebody closed it," Luke said in an awe-filled voice.

"It was an accident," Mary said, sighing.

Samantha hated the thought of a murderer being within walking distance from them again. "Do you think he could be hiding in the passage?"

Luke snorted. "Why the hell would he bother to hide? He's probably walking up the main street right now, holding his sides from laughing, with his pockets stuffed with watches, billfolds, and diamonds. And kicking six tires ahead of him."

"He has only half the diamonds," Samantha pointed out. "He could want to get the rest of them back."

"It's not likely he'd risk it," Sol said.

Mary patted Samantha's hand, "He's sure to be half-

153

way across Ireland by now, knowing the men are out in force looking for him here."

"Oh, I hope so," Samantha said fervently.

"And where are the diamonds you've recovered?" Mary asked curiously.

Luke pulled the pouch from his pocket and tossed it on the table. "There they are."

"Of course there they are," Samantha said, awash with guilt for her earlier suspicions of him.

Luke gave her an assessing eye. "What'd you think? That I'd stashed them away for myself?" he said heavily.

Not really, she told herself. Or had she? Or would she have cared if he had? Very much, she discovered. Not for the loss of the stones themselves but because she couldn't bear the thought of Luke doing such a thing. She couldn't bear the thought of his going off without her either. She shoved the pouch aside. "Would you really go off and leave . . . us?"

"I've got work to do, remember?" He pushed the pouch back in front of her. "Check your stones."

"What for? I trust you." She shoved the pouch aside again. "How can you worry more about making money than what happens to . . . people?"

"I'm not worried about making money, I'm worried about losing it. When I get that problem out of the way, I'll worry about people." He tapped the pouch. "Here, never mind your great faith in me. Reilly could've taken the stones and left the wadding, you know."

"Did he?" she said, unable to muster proper concern for Warren's stones in light of Luke's imminent departure.

"How the hell do I know? Check and see."

All at once everything closed in on her. She flung the pouch across the table. "Diamonds! Diamonds! Is that all you can think about? I'm so sick of those diamonds!

They've brought nothing but trouble. We could all wind up in jail because of them. And—" Tears welled up, and she knew she was letting herself get carried away but she didn't care. "—and two men are dead," she wailed.

"Oh, my God, don't," Luke begged with the panic-stricken helplessness of a man facing a woman's tears.

Mary jumped up and ran around to her. "Now, now," she crooned. "Don't be blaming Reilly's death on the diamonds. There was bad blood between the Reillys and Coffeys—"

"A Reilly killed a Coffey last fall." Sol said.

"And the Amsterdam killing was for some other stones and had nothing to do with these, so there's no need to cry," Luke said in the authoritative voice of one putting things in perspective.

Samantha blinked back the tears. It was a relief—a surprisingly big one—to learn that the diamonds were not responsible for the spilling of blood, but other facts remained. "But we could still wind up in jail because of them," she said.

"They'll have a tough time getting me in jail," Luke said, looking at Samantha. "Even though it means doing our child out of a whale of a story."

"I'm—I'm sorry about that. It just sort of popped out."

"Be sure you tell that to Mr. Donegal. And on that subject, what happened to your high resolve to come clean with him?"

"I simply couldn't bring myself to do it. I keep thinking they'll catch the real criminals," she said miserably.

"And they will. So leave her alone." Mary said.

Luke's sigh washed his hands of both of them.

Mary sat down and fingered the pouch. "I've never seen a whole packet of diamonds."

"Go on and check them, will you please, Samantha," Luke said.

Five stones glittered up at them from the cotton pouch. At least Warren would have something to show for his money. She undid the buttons of her waistband and took a deep breath while Mary and Sol peppered her with questions she couldn't answer. There had been fourteen stones in all, she remembered, and the bill of sale gave the individual descriptions and values of each, but she did not know the weight or value of these particular ones nor had she any idea whether the missing ones were larger or smaller. When they had looked their fill, she gathered the stones back into the pouch and held it out to Luke. "Keep them for me, will you?"

"I don't want the responsibility. Better put them back in your First National Chest."

"I'll look lopsided," she said, looking down at herself, and became aware for the first time that she looked as though she had been dragged around an old secret passageway. Dirty, ripped, and wrinkled, her clothes were a mess. Samantha Malloy, universal favorite, cringed and thought longingly of her suitcase in Parknasilla, wishing she could kick Warren. "Mary, I've got to buy some clothes. . . ."

Mary looked doubtful "The Emporium is the only place we have, but I'm thinking you will not be finding much selection. Maybe we could sponge and press—"

"No, I need something else. This damp weather must shrink wool. I can hardly breathe in this skirt."

"Maybe it's twins," Luke said dryly. But he was very much in favor of going to the Emporium. "Just on the outside chance the phones are working."

"What will you do if they are?" Mary asked warily.

"Get somebody on the jobsite to throw a boat on a truck and come get me."

Samantha, Mary, and Sol all sighed.

"Not that I really expect the phones'll be working, of course," Luke added.

When they arrived at the Emporium, Luke looked up and down the empty street with ill-concealed disgust. Though it was getting on to late afternoon, Riverford held the same unmoving early-morning stillness they had found on their previous visit.

"There's a meeting being held," Mary said, unlocking the door of the Emporium.

"As good a reason as any, I gather, to keep an Irishman from working," Luke said and tramped on through to the telephone, leaving Samantha and Mary and Sol gazing after him dejectedly.

They need not have worried because, of course, the telephones were not working. Luke slammed the receiver down and took in the relieved faces beaming his way. He settled on Mary's. "I'll be damned if you people don't beat me. If nobody in Riverford cares that it's cut off from the outside world, I'd think somebody out there would worry about you."

"Why should they be doing that?" Mary looked genuinely surprised. "Everyone's knowing we've plenty of food for the table and fuel for the fires."

"And more important," Sol said, "that there's plenty for all at the pub."

"The pub? Riverford has a pub?" Luke said.

"Certainly there's a pub. This is Ireland, man. Wherever there's a handful of cottages, you'll find a pub. Riverford's pub is the O'Callaghan Brothers' kitchen. The eldest is the publican. The shelves are fully stocked and there's a nice open hearth, even a television set to watch the football matches if you've a mind to," Sol said.

157

Samantha started. "Television? You have television?"

"At the pub," Mary said. "But the women are welcome only during the day. At night it's strictly all-male, though—" She broke off, her eyes widening. "Oh, dear. . . ."

"Yes," Samantha said mournfully, "oh, dear." She brightened almost immediately. "But it doesn't matter, does it? There's no electricity."

Sol and Mary looked uncomfortable.

"There is electricity?" Samantha asked.

"No, but the set is battery-powered," Sol said. "Mary got it in London for Riverford so the villagers could watch the matches no matter what the weather."

"Now I *know* you should've told Mr. Donegal," Luke told Samantha. "It's a wonder he hasn't seen a broadcast about you."

"For one thing," Sol said, "programming is a little different here than in the States. And for another, he's been pretty busy today. The only thing is—"

"Yes?" Samantha said, not liking the way Mary quickly stepped to her side.

"The only thing is, the meeting's being held at the pub," Sol finished.

"But it's to do with the problem of the tinker, so it's not likely they'll be watching television," Mary said.

"In the short time I've been here, there's one thing I've discovered and that is that you people never do the likely thing," Luke said. "Come on, Sol, let's go take a look at the rivers."

Samantha watched them leave, wondering if Luke would try to swim out of Riverford. She turned away. A body could stand just so much anxiety. And there was nothing like shopping for clothes to take a woman's mind off her troubles.

It took but a glance for her to see that Mary had said

a mouthful when she warned that the Emporium did not have much of a selection. Though she had not expected to find Sybil Connolly creations hanging on the racks, she had been thinking along the lines of soft Irish woolens, fine linens, and lace.

What she found were sprigged cottons that must have been around since the Great Revolution and an assortment of good durable stuff with warmth as its uppermost selling point. The only thing that came close to her size was in the odd-lot of souvenirs Hugh had stocked on the chance that a flood of tourists would descend upon Riverford eager for bright green skirts sprinkled with shamrocks made out of some fluorescent stuff. Samantha eyed the garments silently.

"Most Riverford women make their everyday clothes and shop in the nearby towns for their Sunday things," Mary said.

"I see," Samantha said.

"Would you like to look at some yardage?"

"I think not."

"Well. . . . " Mary spread her hands, helplessly.

"Well. . . ." Samantha sighed. "Well, the cottons and that serge-looking stuff are out, so it'll have to be a green skirt. Maybe I can get the shamrocks unglued."

They were contemplating this unlikely possibility when Luke and Sol returned.

"Are they going down?" Samantha asked, prepared for the worst.

"If you're talking about the bridges, yes," Luke said.

"What about the rivers?" Mary said.

"They're going down," Sol said.

"And taking the bridges with them," Luke said. "Beats me why they're still standing. I wouldn't even take a chance crossing them on foot, as much as I want to get out of here." He shoved his hands in his pockets and moved away.

Samantha controlled the impulse to break into a jig. She happily watched him wandering aimlessly around the counters, then turned back to Mary. "Now," she said briskly, "where's the lingerie?"

"Lingerie? What we have here is underwear."

And so it was. Good sensible stuff, designed to cover up and last. So were the shoes.

"Even Dierdre shops in the nearby towns for her things," Mary said. "Hugh sells mostly—"

"Hallelujah! Ha-lay-loo-yah!" Luke's joyful cry filled the Emporium, and Samantha's mouth fell open as he scrambled onto a counter and reached for a shelf high up on the wall. "What in the world?" she exclaimed.

He tugged a large box from the shelf. "A boat!" he said.

"A boat?" she wailed.

"A boat!" He jumped down. "A beautiful, inflatable raft!" He slapped dust off the box and read out in a glad voice, " 'Two-man raft. Neoprene rubberized canvas resists oil, sun, water. Two air chambers inflate separately. Molded rubber oarlocks. Inflated dimensions: six feet nine inches,' and so forth and so forth and so forth. How about that!"

"That boat's been on the shelf a long time," Mary said bleakly.

"Could be rotted," Sol said.

"It'll probably sink," Samantha said.

But they couldn't dim Luke's spirits. He slammed the box down and reached into his pockets. It was then his face fell. "Hell, I haven't any money. Reilly got my wallet."

"Then I guess you haven't got a boat," Samantha said, not really believing the lack of money would prevent Luke from taking the boat. And it occurred to her she had no money either. "I haven't any money either," she said to Mary. "I can't pay for these clothes."

"It's all right. You both can pay whenever," Mary said dispiritedly. "Hugh won't care."

Samantha couldn't imagine why she felt like crying so much today. "Everyone's so nice here."

"Yes, Riverford's a nice little village with real kind people," Sol said. He looked at Luke.

Mary and Samantha looked at Luke.

Luke threw up his hands. "Goddamn it, I can't carry the world's burdens. I've got my own, you know."

"Yeah," Sol said.

Mary said nothing.

Samantha said nothing.

They rode back to the cottage in silence, Samantha staring at her feet until she heard Luke whisper, "Oh Jesus." She looked up to see Sean Ward's truck in front of Sol's cottage. Standing just beyond it was Mr. Donegal with a notebook in his hand. He was looking from it to the license plate of her little hired car.

CHAPTER XVIII

"I'll just stash this down here for the time being," Luke said, shoving the boxed raft onto the floor of the car as Mary pulled up to the cottage.

They climbed out, lined up, and waited while Mr. Donegal's cold blue eyes raked each one in turn. Samantha hugged her parcels. Sol and Mary moved closer to each other. Luke folded his arms.

"All of you here, are you? Good. Shall we be going inside then?" Mr. Donegal led the way—a man in complete control and relishing it.

They followed him into the kitchen, no one saying anything, while Sol threw blocks of turf onto the grate and set a match to them. The fire caught, crackled, and popped, and though it cast a cheerful warmth, it failed to brighten the spirit of those in the room. Samantha set her parcels down and glumly watched the blaze, as though a tongue of flame might spell out the formula for her deliverance. She didn't bother to remove her coat or the headscarf she wore in lieu of the lost oilskin. Why bother when she'd be hustled off to jail within minutes?

Mr. Donegal's eye lassoed Sol and roped him front and center. "The car in front is not yours," he stated flatly.

"No, sir."

"You allowed me to think it so."

"Yes, sir." Sol stood head bowed as though waiting for the buttons to be stripped off his shirt and the poker wrenched from his hands.

But Mr. Donegal dismissed him and took on Luke. "The young lady is not your wife."

162

"She is not my wife."

"She is not having your child."

"She is definitely not having my child."

"You allowed me to think it so."

"You chose to and—"

Mr. Donegal would have none of it. "You allowed me to think it so, sir," he repeated firmly.

Luke set his jaw. "If you say so."

"And you, Mary, you were aware of all this."

"Yes, Father."

"And conspired to keep it from me."

"Yes, Father."

Sol took a step away from the fireplace. "Don't blame her—"

"Ah, you put her up to it, did you?"

Samantha's head was buzzing with inner voices shrieking orders at her to speak up, but try as she might, her tongue wouldn't come unglued from the roof of her mouth.

"Well—well—" Sol stammered.

Luke threw Samantha a commanding look. "No, it wasn't his fault—"

"Ah, Mr. Carter—or is it Mr. Carter?"

"It's Carter, all right. But Sol's not to blame—"

"Ah, so you've the blame."

"Hell, no. You see—"

"It's my fault! It's all my fault!" The words burst forth from Samantha's lips.

Mr. Donegal looked at her for the first time since they had gathered in the kitchen. "And why would you be saying so?"

"I begged them not to tell you," she said, taking a deep breath and plunging ahead. "I didn't do it, Mr. Donegal. I didn't steal any diamonds and I didn't murder that poor man in Amsterdam." She willed herself not to cry. "I was there, but I was buying diamonds—

not stealing them. Only—only I've lost the bill of sale. But I'm innocent. I swear I'm innocent."

"And that I'm sure of," Mr. Donegal said calmly.

It took a split second for the words to register, but when they did, Samantha fell onto a chair, stunned. "You are?" she said.

"What the hell?" Luke said.

Sol dropped the poker.

And Mary gave a glad little cry and flung her arms around her father.

"Here, here." Mr. Donegal peeled his daughter off him. "Now, none of that. I'm not forgetting where your loyalties lie."

"No such thing," Mary said. "It was just that you had much on your mind and it seemed best simply to let the real criminals be caught first. And they were, were they not? So where's the harm?"

"Ah, but they've not been caught."

Once again shock ran through the room.

"But—but—" Samantha drew a breath and began again. "You've said you know I'm innocent—"

"I've said I'm *sure* you are. A pretty Irish lass—" He peered at her from under bushy brows. "And it is you are Irish, now? A Malooly?"

"Yes," she said, liking the friendly tone of his voice.

"And would they be the Maloolys of Galway, now?"

She could see from his expression that the Galway Maloolys counted and she tried to remember where her grandfather's roots were, but her brain seemed turned to sand. "I'm not sure," she said, opting for honesty as a change of pace and hoping it wouldn't spoil things.

It didn't. "Ah, well, if you're a Malooly, there's bound to be the connection along the way." His smile patted her on the head.

"Mr. Donegal, aside from your unshakable faith in the Irish, I suppose there was something in the television broadcast you saw that suggested the blame for the crime lay elsewhere," Luke said. "Who have they got—"

"Television? I've not seen any television broadcast. It was the newspaper I saw. There are sketches, Miss Malooly, according to descriptions given artists. Though artists being what they are"—his look ticked off Sol—"they bear little resemblance to you. If it'd not been for the hire-car agent supplying the license number . . ." He let that thought hang on the air. "There is also a picture of a young lady from New York who is missing, and there's foolish talk the two young women are actually one."

"It's true, Mr. Donegal," Samantha said.

Mr. Donegal took this in.

"Her story's pretty fascinating. In case you're ever interested in hearing it, of course," Luke said.

"Ah, now you're concerned that I hear it, are you, Mr. Carter? And did it never occur to you earlier?"

"Yes, it occurred to me."

"But you did nothing about it, did you?"

"Are you laying the groundwork for something, Mr. Donegal?"

"Me, Mr. Carter?"

"You, Mr. Donegal."

"Not at all, Mr. Carter." He turned to Samantha. "I was thinking you could do with a cup of tea first, though something stronger would be better for you if it were offered. And then I'll be hearing your story."

"I'll just be getting the whiskey," Sol said.

When the drinks were poured, Samantha accepted hers with an enthusiasm that raised Luke's eyebrows, but she felt that if ever there was a day she deserved to get pie-eyed, this was it. She gulped down a mouthful and then had another.

"Better get on with it—while you can," Luke said.

She took a deep breath and got on with it, stumbling along, backtracking, and always careful to designate Warren simply as a friend. She sensed that their true relationship would not sit well with the Irishman's concept of what was fitting and proper and she dared not risk wiping out the sympathetic gleam in Mr. Donegal's eye. When she'd finished, she sat back, full of the sense of virtue and lightness that confession brings.

"She forgot to mention that there were cleaners in front of VanDam's house," Luke said. "Did the cab-driver tell about the two guys with the old truck who were coiling hoses when they pulled up? Because they were still there coiling hoses when she left. And that's a long time spent coiling hoses. Particularly when there was no sign of anything having been hosed down. If you ask me, they're the ones the police should be looking for."

"Know quite a bit about it, don't you, Mr. Carter?"

"No more than the others here," Luke said. "So don't go—" He broke off and frowned. "Just a minute. Newspaper? How did you get hold of a newspaper? With the bridges down?"

"Ah, that. Well now, one of my men brought it a bit ago when he rowed over thinking to take me back. I couldn't leave, of course."

"But he has. Left, I mean. With the boat, of course," Luke said. "It's a wonder there isn't a traffic jam with all the rowing back and forth. And never a trip for me, is that it?"

"We were hoping you'd decide to stay as we asked. And now we're thinking you will."

"Oh? And why would you be thinking that?"

" 'Tis a serious matter your not informing the authorities of Miss Malooly's whereabouts. Authorities in this case being myself."

"But it was my fault that he kept quiet," Samantha said, pushing her luck.

"Sure it was only natural for you to behave so. But it doesn't make him the less guilty."

"It doesn't?" Samantha said.

"While you're passing the guilt around, what about the others?" Luke asked heavily.

"Womenfolk cannot be expected to judge the fitting and proper thing to do." His tone brought a glint to Mary's eye, but she tightened her lips. "And this one"—he jerked a thumb at Sol—"ah well. . . ." His shrug took care of Sol. "But you, sir, a man of your reach and intelligence. . . ." He shook his head.

"Okay, Mr. Donegal, you've worked up to something. Spill it."

"Me, Mr. Carter?"

"You, Mr. Donegal."

"Not so, Mr. Carter. 'Tis the international police I'm worrying about. Rigid men they are. Never considering the circumstances, only the job."

"And you, Mr. Donegal?"

"Well now, Mr. Carter, I believe circumstances have some to do with the situations people find themselves placed in."

"Shall we get down to particular situations, Mr. Donegal? Mine, for instance. The one you find me in, Mr. Donegal, not the one the international police might assume."

"Ah, I was that right about your intelligence, was I?"

Samantha gave up trying to follow the conversation. She threw up her hands. "I can't make head or tails out of what you're saying."

"What it boils down to is that you're off the hook," Luke said grimly.

"I am?"

"And I'm on it. Right, Mr. Donegal?"

"Well now, 'tis more like I'm thinking you might re-consider helping Riverford get around a situation that's beyond its capabilities."

"And if I don't?"

"You've a reputation in business circles that might be jarred somewhat if it was known you obstructed jus-tice."

"If you really believe that, you sure don't know what's going on in the outside world, Mr. Donegal. No-body'd blink an eye over small potatoes like that in this day and age."

"Well then, supposing we say you're a busy man and being tied up fighting accusations for weeks or months would affect the smooth running of your business."

Luke looked as though he'd like to punch somebody. Hard. "Try it and I'll sue everybody, governments and all, if I have to. And I'd recoup any losses, you can bet."

"Ah, but we'd be very careful only to suggest, Mr. Carter, only suggest complicity. And you must admit there's enough of the truth to it to give it strength."

Luke's face chilled and emptied. "Looks like you've got me over a barrel, doesn't it, Mr. Donegal?" he said, lightly enough.

Mr. Donegal took his measure for a moment, then pushed back from the table. "I'll be telling that you've decided to help us, then?"

"Tell them anything you like, Mr. Donegal," Luke said smugly, thinking of his inflatable boat.

Mr. Donegal eyed him a moment more, then nodded briskly, downed his drink, and took off, looking about ten feet tall.

"Will someone please tell me what that was all about," Samantha said.

"It's very simple. Neat and simple," Luke said. "All

I'm supposed to do is take the rap for that tinker's death and Mr. Donegal'll let the authorities assume he was properly notified by all concerned in the Amsterdam matter."

"And where's the harm?" Mary asked softly.

"The harm is . . . the harm is . . . oh, hell!" Luke got up and paced around the room.

Samantha watched him, not forgetting for one moment that he had the means to leave Riverford. It would make no difference to her position now, so there was nothing personal in her wanting him to stay, she told herself. It was for Riverford's sake. *Oh, yeah?* a small voice whispered. But there was no denying she found herself enormously concerned with the fate of Riverford.

Luke came back to the table. "How long would this farce take?"

Everyone brightened.

"The hearing shouldn't last an hour," Sol said.

"Okay, let's go. If they're having a meeting now, we might just as well get it over with. I can wait an hour to leave, I guess."

"But it's not possible," Mary said.

"Why not?" Luke asked.

"Why not?" Samantha asked, coming unbrightened again.

"The Reilly family must be sent for and—"

"So how long can that take? Send a message on any one of the dozen boats rowing in and out of the village," Luke snapped.

"But it's getting on to dark and there's no telling where to look for them."

"They were just down the road—" Samantha began.

"Which is not to say they're still there. They could have gone up to the fork, searching."

Luke threw up his hands. "For once just get on with

169

it, will you? Better yet, I'll do it myself. Where's this meeting?"

Sol scrambled to his feet. "At the pub. Mary . . . ?"

"No, it's better you men go. They—they don't like women in the pub at night."

When they had gone off, Mary said, "It'll never work, you know. That's why I thought it best that we stay here."

"What won't work?"

"Pushing the council. All the members aren't there, and there is a touchiness about making decisions without all present."

"How long would it take to get them all together?"

"A day or so, I'm thinking. The storm, you know. Fences must be mended, roofs must be patched, and crops, tended."

"Luke won't like that."

"Just why I chose not to go with them. He does roar, doesn't he."

"He's going to roar right out of Riverford in his rubber raft, I think," Samantha said.

She had pegged it all right.

Luke came storming into the cottage. "I can't believe these people," he bellowed. "Well, they had their chance and they blew it. I'm getting my stuff together and getting out of here." He stomped out of the room.

Samantha sighed, Mary sighed, and Sol sighed. Sol placed a newspaper on the table in front of Samantha. "Thought you might like to see this," he said.

Two sketches and a photograph nicely balanced a blazing headline: MYSTERY BLONDE IDENTIFIED. The sketch artists had done a bang-up job of capturing her likeness. They might have worked from the Wirephoto alongside. But how could they have done otherwise when provided with descriptions by a birdwatcher and two observant priests? Warren must be in a state of shock.

Samantha shoved the paper aside and propped her chin in her hand.

After a while Mary said, "Lots of shouting, was there?"

"No, none as a matter fact."

"Luke didn't go in?" Samantha asked.

"Oh, yes, he went in. He sort of rumbled when they said they couldn't have an official council meeting right now. And he was real patient while he told them it had to be now or not at all. A little muscle in his jaw was working pretty fast. But he was patient. He paced a lot while they explained how it was and he paced a lot while he explained how it had to be. But he didn't yell."

"He might even get used to us," Samantha said, "if he stays in Ireland long enough."

They were still sitting at the table when Luke came in. He stopped at the table. "I know what you're all thinking and I suppose I don't blame you. But I can't stick around here any longer."

"We understand. It's all right," Samantha said.

He looked at her, and then looked away. He did a lot of that until he decided it was dark enough to leave.

"I'll drive you," Sol said.

"Are you coming?" Luke asked Samantha.

"No, I think I'll just say good-bye here."

"Okay, well, there's no point dragging it out. Good-bye, Mary." He shook her hand. "Sorry I have to do this." He stood looking down at Samantha's shorn head. "Samantha . . . I'll—I'll get in touch, okay?"

"Okay," she said, not looking up. Not daring to.

And he was gone. She had never felt so miserable in her whole life.

CHAPTER XIX

Sol wasn't gone very long. He came into the room, sighed, said it looked like the rain was over, handed the car keys to Mary, and said he thought the car was getting low on petrol. Then he blew out a breath and said, well, the coast had been clear and Luke had got off all right. Mary sighed and Samantha said she thought she'd lie down.

Once in the bedroom, Samantha found it impossible to lie down. Instead, she stood at the window for a time, looking out at nothing. Then she paced around the room for a while. She stopped at the other window and stood looking out of that one at nothing. Then she paced around the room again. It was a pattern she followed for what might have been ten minutes or ten hours for all she knew. She seemed to be a disembodied spirit—like Chagall figures floating above never-never land. When Mary knocked and came in, Samantha tried to bring her into focus.

Mary took one look, quickly crossed the room, and put her arms around Samantha. "Oh, Samantha," she said. And it was like the key log slipping the jam. The tears burst forth.

When Sol came inquiringly to the doorway, Samantha was still crying and Mary was crooning and patting her shoulder. He blanched and started to back away, but Mary spotted him. "You . . . men . . ." she said darkly.

He winced but came in.

Mary smoothed back Samantha's hair. "Now, now, Samantha, you'll be feeling better now for the tears, and there's none who'll say you haven't the right to them. But I'm thinking you'll be making yourself sick if there's more crying. And all for the likes of him that doesn't deserve them."

"Now just a minute, Mary," Sol said, frowning. "You can't blame Luke for thinking his own problems are more important than those of people he's known for less than twenty-four hours."

Samantha lifted her head. Less than twenty-four hours? It couldn't be. But it was. And Sol was right. She wiped her eyes. "You're right, Sol," she said in a teary voice.

Mary tossed her head. "Well . . ."

Sol gave her a look.

"Well . . . I'll make a pot of tea. Come on, Samantha, there's nothing like a—" She caught herself, looked at the two of them, and then bristled. "Well, there isn't."

The tears were dried by the time Mary poured the tea.

"Father will have to be told of Luke's going," Mary said after they'd sat around the table, silently sipping for some minutes.

"I know," Sol said gloomily.

"We'd better give Luke a little more time to get further away," Samantha said in an empty voice.

"I suppose so," Mary said. "There's a bit of loaf left. Would anyone be wanting a slice?"

Samantha didn't want any, nor did Sol. Mary drummed her fingers on the table. Then she said, "Maybe I'll just mix up a batch or two of bread. I'll show you how, Samantha. It'll give us something to do."

But Samantha had been thinking. She waved Mary's suggestion aside. "I'll tell your father that Luke has gone. And I'll tell him there's no use trying to go after him to force him to do as Riverford wishes because I'll

173

swear he didn't know anything. I'll tell the newspapers Luke is being victimized if the council won't listen to me. I'm sure Riverford doesn't want that kind of publicity. Not if they expect any tourists to come here."

"You're Irish, all right," Sol said.

"So then, I'll shower and change and we'll go face them."

And in short order she had showered and changed into her new-bought finery, without batting an eye at the glowing shamrocks, the homespun blouse, or the heavy serviceable sweater. "Maybe it'll start a whole new style" was all she said when Mary and Sol eyed her.

Sol and Mary followed the gleaming shamrocks down the cinder path to the car. Twilight was slipping into evening. Small clouds scudded across the darkening sky, but there was no mist or drizzle, and Samantha was glad that Luke was spared a rainy trek up whatever road he was trekking up.

They got into the car, but nothing happened when Mary turned the key.

"It did that with me too," Sol said.

"Bang the dashboard," Samantha said.

"Maybe it's out of fuel," Mary said, peering.

"You're low, but the gauge says there's still some in the tank," Sol said.

"It isn't always true," Mary said. "I've told Father to get it fixed, but he says he knows when it's near empty." She tried the ignition again; it caught and they drove off.

At the pub Mr. Donegal and the village men frowned and pursed their lips at the sight of the women.

"Mary, you're knowing the evening is not—" Mr. Donegal began.

Samantha quickly took the wind out of his and the others' sails with the news of their scapegoat's escape.

174

Then she began to lay down the law. If anyone was going to be thrown to the wolves, it was she because what did it matter anyway? "When they come rowing across the river to get me, they might as well put me in jail for a tinker's murder I didn't commit along with the diamond merchant's murder I didn't commit."

But the Irishmen would have none of it. First off, she was not going to go to any jail because "they" would not be rowing across any river to get her. All "they" knew was that she had left Cork and disappeared on the way to Parknasilla. "And who would be thinking to look for her in Riverford?" Mr. Donegal wanted to know. It was unanimously agreed by all around the table that no one ever thought of Riverford.

And as for Riverford, why, what man here knew what she was talking about, cut off from the outside world as they were? "If a Malooly—and a Galway Malooly, you're remembering—" Everyone assured Mr. Donegal that he remembered. "If a Malooly should be in the neighborhood, where is the surprise that she should visit old friends of the family? And there are many of these in Riverford, to be sure." There was much nodding and aying around the table. "And once here, how was the innocent lamb or anyone else to know she was causing a stir elsewhere? Riverford being so isolated by the storm and all."

And they would hear no more about it for there was the problem of Reilly to tackle again.

"I'm thinking," Sol said, setting his jaw and ignoring the disbelieving eyes of those around the table, "if I go to Reilly's caravan and tell his family that I found him breaking into my cottage to steal Samantha's diamonds and we fought and I hit him and he fell on his knife . . . ?

The men thought that over, looking to one another from time to time to see if there were any dissenting faces. But everyone was nodding to himself, apparently liking the idea once they got used to its having come from Sol.

But of course they weren't going to come flat out and agree to it. "Well now, let's discuss this possibility," Mr. Donegal said.

Samantha let out a sigh. That was that.

"Do you want to stay?" Mary asked her.

"Not really."

"If you're not wanting to stay," Mr. Donegal said, "I'll be taking Sol home when we've finished here."

"You girls run along," Sol said, and turned to the men. "And I'll be buying for the house."

The men nodded at this good idea, and the eldest got out a full bottle and another glass.

"Sit down, Sol," Mr. Donegal said, and Sol sat down, the others moving closer to him. Mr. Donegal poured.

"Now then," Mr. Donegal said, "here's what you'll be saying. . . ."

Mary and Samantha filed out the door.

The night was still clear, and a pale moon slid in and out of small clouds. Samantha pulled her sweater closer as they walked to the car. She hoped Luke got a ride.

They got into the car, and Mary said, "We could go to Dierdre's if you like and maybe have a bit of dinner with her."

"I'd rather not, Mary. I really don't feel like visiting just now."

"Of course," Mary said and put the car in gear.

It sputtered as they passed Dierdre's house and again when they'd made the turn. Just beyond O'Sullivan House it stopped.

Mary fiddled with the ignition for a bit, but the engine did not respond. "Well, I can nip back and borrow someone else's car."

"It's only a short way to the cottage. Let's walk," Samantha said. "When your father brings Sol home, he can do something about the car."

Mary saw nothing wrong with the idea and got a flashlight from the glove compartment. They climbed out of the car and started down the road. The shamrocks on Samantha's skirt lit up the night almost as much as the flashlight, which Mary shone just ahead of their feet to point out the pools of rainwater and patches of deep mud.

Samantha skirted just such a puddle and almost tripped over feet lying just outside the pool. "Oh, my God, another body!" she cried, trying to regain her balance.

Mary flashed the light back. "Mother of God! I think it's Luke!" she gasped.

And it was. If Samantha hadn't skirted the puddle, they might have gone right past without seeing him lying there, facedown, mostly on the verge.

"Luke!" Samantha flung herself down beside him and turned him over. He groaned and looked up cross-eyed at her.

"Luke! Luke!" she wailed, trying to cradle his head while he weakly tried to fight off her hands. "Are you all right? Luke, please say you're all right. Luke, please, please say something!"

"Samantha, you're smothering me."

His voice was groggy but authoritative enough to convince her he wasn't breathing his last. She abandoned his head to help him sit up, "Careful, careful," she begged.

Mary got down beside them. "What happened?"

"Somebody hit me from behind." Luke felt the back of his head.

"Who was it?" Samantha asked, her hands exploring along with his.

"He didn't say." Luke let out a yelp. "Samantha, for God's sake take it easy. That hurt."

Mary played the light on the back of his head.

"It's a bump the size of an egg," Samantha said.

"I could've told you that, you didn't have to poke at it." He gingerly felt the lump again. "I'll tell you one thing, I'm getting tired of people around here hitting me on the head."

"Do you want to get up?" Mary asked.

"Well, I don't plan on sitting here all night, that's for sure. Samantha, please let go of my head so I can get up."

"Here, let us help you," Samantha said. "Mary, put the flashlight down and take his other arm."

"No, don't. I can—Samantha, watch it, you're going to kick that flash—Oh, great," he said as the flashlight rolled a few feet and clicked off. "Please, I can make it by myself." But they would have none of it, and he finally stood up despite them. He shook them off. "Just let me get my bearings. Please?"

Samantha took a step back onto the verge. Mary retrieved the flashlight. Luke breathed a couple of deep breaths and stood, trying his neck and shoulder muscles in a series of gyrations.

Mary swung the light back on him. "Oh, dear. Luke, your clothes are a—Why, where's Samantha?"

"Samantha?" Luke looked around to where Samantha had been. "Samantha?" he called out. There was no answer. "Samantha," he roared into the night.

CHAPTER XX

Samantha heard him but could do little about answering with a large smelly hand clamped over her mouth as she was dragged through tall grasses and undergrowth.

She lashed out with arms, elbows, and good stout shoes and heard the satisfying sound of a heel cracking against bone. The fellow cursed, his hand slipped, and she yelled with all her might. She heard Luke shout, "I'm coming, Samantha," and with a burst of energy she bit down hard when the hand clapped back over her mouth. The fellow yelled with pain, and she reached back to rake his face with her long nails. He yelled again, his hold slipping. She wrenched out of his grasp and started running in the direction of Luke's bellowing. In a moment she ran smack into his arms.

He held her tight for an instant, then panted, "Come on," and, gripping her hand, took off.

There was enough moon for her to see that they were in the overgrown gardens of O'Sullivan House. Running through tall grass and tangles of bracken and shrubs, into trees and bushes, tripping, slipping, and scrambling to keep their footing; Samantha thought surely her heart was going to bang itself right out of her chest. If she fell once more, she would never get up. Then she did stumble and indeed couldn't get up. She lay where she had fallen, gasping and gulping for air.

Luke fought for breath too as he said, "Get up, Samantha, please get up. We can't stay here. That skirt. Like a goddamned beacon."

The shamrocks were glowing all right. It was a wonder they didn't attract moths. But she couldn't get up. She simply couldn't.

"Please, please, Samantha." Luke pulled at her dead weight. "Samantha, I can hear him. Good God, he's coming."

In an instant they were again crashing through tall grass, bracken, and shrubs, and then Luke swung her around and into the middle of a low-growing clump of something. Cautioning her with an unnecessary "Shshsh"—she couldn't have uttered a word if her life depended on it—He gathered her into his arms. At the rate it was beating, Samantha was certain her heart couldn't last another second, but she thought it was a lovely way to go.

Then the fellow's footsteps pounded close, around and about them. Luke's arms tightened. Neither of them breathed. The footsteps thudded past. Luke relaxed his hold. "Are you all right?" he whispered in her ear.

She nodded into his chest. These days "all right" meant you were still in one piece. "Who is it?" she whispered back.

"The guy who killed Reilly, I'll bet. After the rest of your diamonds," he said against her ear.

She wondered why he had attacked Luke, but then the footsteps came pounding up again and there was the sound of thrashing about, and Luke held her even tighter and now she was really frightened. The fellow had killed once today; two more murders would probably mean nothing to him. She was certain he would hear her heart thumping.

But it wasn't her heartbeat he honed in on; it was the glow of the shamrocks. With a triumphant roar he crashed into the bushes, making a grab for her skirt. Luke lashed out a foot. As the fellow shrieked with pain and fell back, Luke yanked her out of the bush and over the hulk, who roared. They were off and run-

180

ning, but in a moment the footsteps were once more pounding close behind.

We're going to be killed, Samantha told herself. And for what? For Warren's diamonds. All this nightmare of running to save their lives and Warren's diamonds. No! She broke her hand loose, snatched out the pouch, and ripped it open.

"Samantha, what are you doing?" Luke made a grab for her.

But she sidestepped him, spun around, shouted, "Here!" and flung the stones at the huge form advancing on their heels. In the same instant lights flashed over the scene, setting the stones ablaze as they rained through the air. The fellow let out a cry and, bringing himself up short, dropped to his knees, clawing through the grass, cursing and moaning.

Luke didn't hesitate. He took three swift strides back to the giant and gave him two quick chops across the back of the neck. The fellow flattened out.

Samantha sagged and Luke's arms went around her as they stood trancelike, looking down at the fellow. Then more cars drove up and they heard Sol and Mary calling their names. Luke called in an exhausted voice, "Over here."

In a moment the place was thick with Irishmen bearing sticks, rocks, shovels, and hammers, with Sol and Mary in the lead. They pulled up short and gazed down. "It's Coffey," Sol said.

Mr. Donegal pushed through to the front. He too looked down, silent for a moment. Then he sighed and said, "And now we've two of them."

Coffey groaned and stirred.

"The way tinkers disappear around here," Luke said, "you won't have this one long if you don't snap the handcuffs on him."

Of course Donegal had no handcuffs. But no matter. Someone handed Sol a rope and he set about tying Coffey's hands behind him while two of the O'Callaghan Brothers sat on his legs and two of them sat on his shoulders. The eldest squatted at his head with a stout stick, threatening him when he moved and complaining about the time Sol was taking and the knots he was using.

When he was done, Sol asked Luke to help him march Coffey off, and all the Irishmen followed slowly, nodding and murmuring to each other, full of the satisfaction that comes with having fought the good fight.

Mr. Donegal came over to Samantha. Mary was clucking over her, smoothing her hair away from her face and patting her.

"Are you all right, then?" Mr. Donegal asked.

"I am," Samantha said, though her voice wavered.

"Good girl. And there's good news for you. They've caught them who murdered and robbed the merchant in Amsterdam. 'Twas them who pretended to be cleaning men, the radio broadcast said."

"That's good." It was all she could think of to say. She was glad, of course, but she hadn't doubted for an instant that they would be caught. Had she? She didn't think so. Now that it was over.

Mr. Donegal shook his head regretfully. "It's a bad time you've had of it here. I'm thinking you'll be glad to see the last of Riverford, though it saddens me to say so."

"No, that's not true. I won't be glad to leave Riverford." Surprising. But she meant it. No matter that her time in Riverford could be counted in hours, she felt as though she'd spent a lifetime here among these remarkable people. She had only met a handful of them, and yet the whole village had been prepared to believe her innocent and give her shelter and friendship. She

182

wanted to meet Dierdre and see the new baby. What was there in New York, after all? Warren? She looked at the cluster of cars among the trees. In the glare of headlights she could see Luke, head and shoulders above the others, trying to get Coffey into Sean Ward's van.

"Came back, did he," Mr. Donegal said.

"Yes, he did," she said.

"I'm wondering why," he said.

"I think the raft probably sank," she said. Why else?

Samantha paused in the doorway of the kitchen while Mary went in. "I'll stir up the fire and put the kettle on and see what there is for a meal," Mary said. "Though there's no telling when they'll be coming back. Luke and Sol, that is."

"I suppose not." Samantha looked around her. Was it only twenty-four hours ago that she had walked into this room?

"It's not that they'll be long over Coffey and Reilly once they've rowed them across and done the telephoning. It won't take long then for the villains to be handed over properly. But who's to say what time they'll be at the pub." She frowned irritably. "I don't know why we were left out of the celebrating. I'll be giving Solomon Leibowitz a piece of my mind, you can be sure. Just men indeed! You've more right than they to be there. You're the one who's been battered and bruised this whole day. Though of course Luke's had his share of knocks."

"Yes, he has," Samantha agreed. The thinking was that Coffey had been headed for the cottage after the other pouch of diamonds when he spied Luke setting out toward the pub. Assuming Luke still had the stones in his pocket, Coffey had attacked him.

Samantha moved into the kitchen.

"You're done in, aren't you," Mary said. "Come sit by the fire. Shall I get you a whiskey?"

"No, I don't want any whiskey. And I don't want to sit. Let me do something. Please."

She was up to her elbows in dough when Luke and Sol arrived.

"What the hell are you doing?" Luke asked in astonishment.

"I'm making soda bread."

"The hell you are."

He came over and stood beside her. She hated the way her heart skipped. "Do you always have to swear so much?" she asked irritably.

"Me? Swear?"

"All the time. It's disgusting." She slapped the sticky dough around the floured board.

"Is it now? Well, I'll try to watch it."

Sol and Mary exchanged glances. Sol nodded, and they tiptoed out of the room. Neither Luke nor Samantha took notice.

"I called Parknasilla and told them you were all right," Luke said. "I thought you might want me to do that."

"That was good of you." She pounded the dough. "And did you call your people to come get you?"

"No." He poked a finger into the dough. "The guy I talked to wanted to know if you'd be in time to do some shots tomorrow. I said I didn't know, that you'd had rather a rough day."

"And that's for sure. Why didn't you call your people?"

"I did earlier. When I crossed on the raft."

She stopped pummeling the dough and stared up at him. "You got across on the raft?"

184

"Certainly, what the—what did you think?"

"I thought it had sunk or something. And that's why you were back. Why did you come back?"

He picked up the dough and slapped it back down onto the board. "That the way you do it?"

"Yes. Luke, why did you come back?"

He shoved the dough around. "Oh . . . I got to thinking about all that blood on the streets of Riverford."

"But that problem no longer existed this last time you were at the phone. Why didn't you ask them to come get you?"

"I gave them all the information they'll need. They can handle it. Did you get all your diamonds?"

"Sean Ward dropped off the ones I threw at Coffey and the pouch that he had taken from Reilly. And the bill of sale. They found it in Coffey's cap. I suppose you're leaving right away for wherever the job is that you have to finish."

"I've got some things to do first." He picked up the dough again and slammed it down. "What's this supposed to do to it?"

"Who knows." She started kneading the dough again. "You've got to take your—your friend's car back to her, don't you? Before you leave, I mean."

"I'll see that she gets it somehow. What about you? When are you going back to New York?"

"I'm thinking of staying here for a while. Mary said I could help her and Sol get started on O'Sullivan House."

"How's Warren going to like that?"

"I haven't any idea."

"Oh?"

"And what's more"—she gave the dough a good punch—"I don't care."

185

"Ah."

She raised her head and looked him straight in the eye. She was a woman who had come to terms with herself. "The diamonds are all he really wants."

He held her eyes. "And what would *you* be really wanting, Mary Samantha Malooly?" he asked softly.

She knew exactly what she wanted. Him. And she knew from the look in his eyes and the sound of his voice that she could have him. Until morning anyway. And then he'd be gone for wherever he was off to. Another place, another woman. And she'd be worse off than before. So she looked away. "All I want is peace and quiet," she said. She wiped her hands on Mary's apron as she walked over to the stove.

He followed her. "Expect to find it in Riverford, do you?"

"At least I have real friends here," she said, opening the oven door a crack and peeking in.

He leaned over and peeked in too. "And what is that in there?"

She gently closed the door. "I've a loaf that's just about done."

"Have you now? And I suppose there'll be a pot of tea to go with it? And a bit of jam, perhaps?"

She quickly glanced at him, but his expression was as innocent as his tone had been. "It's likely," she said carefully, not certain he wasn't laughing at her.

He followed her back to the table. "You're really settling in, aren't you?"

She attacked the lump of dough. "And why not?" she said, conscious of his nearness and wishing he'd leave now because she wasn't sure how much longer she could hold out.

"That's what I say. Why not? I feel kind of Erin Go Bragh myself, you know."

He moved closer, and she gave the dough a bang

and then flattened it and put her soul into working it into a circular shape. "I find that hard to believe," she said, hating the way her voice trembled.

"Believe it."

He was so close, her arm grazed him as she picked up a knife and cut a wobbly X on the top of the dough.

"Aren't you wondering why I'm not leaving right away?" he asked.

"Something to do with lack of transportation, I suppose," she said, putting the dough on a floured tin.

"Not so. It's the bridges. I've been asked to stay on and do something about replacing them."

Her heart leaped. She turned to face him, the tin in her hands. "And what did you say to that?"

He brushed flour off her cheek. "Oh, I said yes, of course. It was just a question of how long it took to settle a couple of problems. And one's already out of the way."

"And then you'll be staying on? In Riverford?" On her best day Mary couldn't have topped the lilt in Samantha's voice.

"I will that."

"And the other job, will it take long to settle its problem?" Nothing could stop the lilt.

"The problems I had in mind weren't on the jobs. I'll be close enough to get to the one on the coast regularly. And I've good men on the other one. I'll look in on them from time to time when you and I can get away."

The tin trembled in her hands. "You and I?" she said like a full chorus singing "Ode to Joy."

He took the tin from her. "Which brings us to the remaining problem—the other having been Warren and he's out of the way. This business of everybody calling you Mrs. Carter—would you be considering taking the name on a permanent basis?"

She felt the grin split her face, and for a moment all

she could do was let it grow wider. Then she said, " 'Tis a bonny idea."

His grin matched hers. "I think that's Scottish," he said.

"Whatever," she said happily.

They moved to each other and found the tin between them. Luke looked down at it. "What do we do with this?"

"Just set it down. We'll be taking the other loaf out in a minute."

He set the tin down and put his arms around her. "And would that be as long as a jiffy, now?"

She slipped her arms around his neck. "I'm thinking it would be."

He drew her close. "And would there be time for kissing?"

"And hugging, I'm thinking."

They grinned at each other for just a moment longer, and then the grins faded and he said softly, "Oh, Samantha," and lowered his head.

And she said, "Oh, Lu—"

And, alas, the loaf burned.

Ah, well. . . .

Love—the way you want it!

Candlelight Romances

			TITLE NO.	
☐	**A MAN OF HER CHOOSING** by Nina Pykare	.$1.50	#554	(15133-3)
☐	**PASSING FANCY** by Mary Linn Roby	.$1.50	#555	(16770-1)
☐	**THE DEMON COUNT** by Anne Stuart	.$1.25	#557	(11906-5)
☐	**WHERE SHADOWS LINGER** by Janis Susan May	.$1.25	#556	(19777-5)
☐	**OMEN FOR LOVE** by Esther Boyd	.$1.25	#552	(16108-8)
☐	**MAYBE TOMORROW** by Marie Pershing	.$1.25	#553	(14909-6)
☐	**LOVE IN DISGUISE** by Nina Pykare	.$1.50	#548	(15229-1)
☐	**THE RUNAWAY HEIRESS** by Lillian Cheatham	.$1.50	#549	(18083-X)
☐	**HOME TO THE HIGHLANDS** by Jessica Eliot	.$1.25	#550	(13104-9)
☐	**DARK LEGACY** by Candace Connell	.$1.25	#551	(11771-2)
☐	**LEGACY OF THE HEART** by Lorena McCourtney	.$1.25	#546	(15645-9)
☐	**THE SLEEPING HEIRESS** by Phyllis Taylor Pianka	.$1.50	#543	(17551-8)
☐	**DAISY** by Jennie Tremaine	.$1.50	#542	(11683-X)
☐	**RING THE BELL SOFTLY** by Margaret James	.$1.25	#545	(17626-3)
☐	**GUARDIAN OF INNOCENCE** by Judy Boynton	.$1.25	#544	(11862-X)
☐	**THE LONG ENCHANTMENT** by Helen Nuelle	.$1.25	#540	(15407-3)
☐	**SECRET LONGINGS** by Nancy Kennedy	.$1.25	#541	(17609-3)

Once you've tasted joy and passion, do you dare dream of

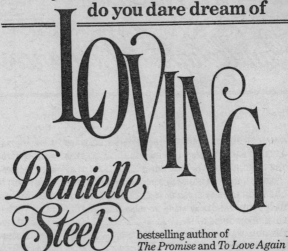

LOVING

Danielle Steel

bestselling author of
The Promise and *To Love Again*

Bettina Daniels lived in a gilded world—pampered, adored, ador-
ing. She had youth, beauty and a glamorous life that circled the
globe—everything her father's love, fame and money could buy.
Suddenly, Justin Daniels was gone. Bettina stood alone before a
mountain of debts and a world of strangers—men who promised
her many things, who tempted her with words of love. But
Bettina had to live her own life, seize her own dreams and take
her own chances. But could she pay the bittersweet price?

A Dell Book ================================ **$2.75 (14684-4)**

Dell BESTSELLERS

- ☐ **TOP OF THE HILL** by Irwin Shaw $2.95 (18976-4)
- ☐ **THE ESTABLISHMENT** by Howard Fast........$3.25 (12296-1)
- ☐ **SHOGUN** by James Clavell $3.50 (17800-2)
- ☐ **LOVING** by Danielle Steel $2.75 (14684-4)
- ☐ **THE POWERS THAT BE**
  by David Halberstam $3.50 (16997-6)
- ☐ **THE SETTLERS** by William Stuart Long $2.95 (15923-7)
- ☐ **TINSEL** by William Goldman $2.75 (18735-4)
- ☐ **THE ENGLISH HEIRESS** by Roberta Gellis....$2.50 (12141-8)
- ☐ **THE LURE** by Felice Picano $2.75 (15081-7)
- ☐ **SEAFLAME** by Valerie Vayle $2.75 (17693-X)
- ☐ **PARLOR GAMES** by Robert Marasco $2.50 (17059-1)
- ☐ **THE BRAVE AND THE FREE**
  by Leslie Waller $2.50 (10915-9)
- ☐ **ARENA** by Norman Bogner $3.25 (10369-X)
- ☐ **COMES THE BLIND FURY** by John Saul $2.75 (11428-4)
- ☐ **RICH MAN, POOR MAN** by Irwin Shaw $2.95 (17424-4)
- ☐ **TAI-PAN** by James Clavell $3.25 (18462-2)
- ☐ **THE IMMIGRANTS** by Howard Fast $2.95 (14175-3)
- ☐ **BEGGARMAN, THIEF** by Irwin Shaw $2.75 (10701-6)

At your local bookstore or use this handy coupon for ordering:

Dell DELL BOOKS
P.O. BOX 1000, PINEBROOK, N.J. 07058

Please send me the books I have checked above. I am enclosing $ _____
(please add 75¢ per copy to cover postage and handling). Send check or money
order—no cash or C.O.D.'s. Please allow up to 8 weeks for shipment.

Mr/Mrs/Miss _____

Address _____

City _____ State/Zip _____